Showdown at Snakebite Creek

Seven years earlier Cole Tibb's father had been murdered alongside Snakebite Creek and now Cole wants justice. He returns to Raven Flats looking to settle the old grudge. But settling a grudge and surviving are two very different things. Soon he finds himself opposing a greedy landowner named Carleton Usher, his ruthless sons, and a merciless group of killers.

The arrival of enigmatic US Marshal Maxfield Knight raises the stakes in a deadly game of survival. As the bodies begin stacking up like firewood Cole realizes he has only two things in his favour – his ruthless determination to set things right and his ability with a gun.

By the same author

Trail of the Burned Man
Wind Rider

Showdown at Snakebite Creek

Thomas McNulty

A Black Horse Western

ROBERT HALE · LONDON

ISBN 978-0-7090-9202-5

Robert Hale Limited
Clerkenwell House
Clerkenwell Green
London EC1R 0HT

www.halebooks.com

With love for Jan and Brenna,
my parents,
and to the memory of my uncle
Robert Bump

Typeset by
Derek Doyle & Associates, Shaw Heath
Printed and bound in Great Britain by
CPI Antony Rowe, Chippenham and Eastbourne

CHAPTER ONE

Pap Wingfoot was sitting in his rocking chair on the board-walk outside of his adobe cantina and watching the blackbirds in the street when he saw the rider in the distance. Flies were buzzing near the outhouse when the rider appeared as a speck on the horizon. Pap's yellow dog, Grant, lifted his head and perked his ears. Pap thought it was high time he showed up and a frown creased his brow. The speck in the distance shimmered like a mirage under the boiling noonday sun.

It won't be long now and this town will sound like the first battle at Bull Run!

Pap had to resist the urge to jump with joy. Of course, the outcome was far from determined, but Pap's instincts told him life was about to change dramatically in the town of Raven Flats. He pulled a corncob pipe from his vest along with a leather pouch of tobacco. He packed the tobacco into the pipe, struck a match, and smoked contentedly as the speck on the horizon grew larger.

Seven long years had passed since Pap had seen the man he now believed was riding in his direction. How the country had changed in that span of time! Custer and

Hickok were dead and old Grant had left the White House for retirement in the east. Bill Cody was in England last he heard, entertaining kings and queens with his traveling Wild West show.

Pap chuckled to himself. Folks nowadays had no idea how wild the west had really been – wild at times, but deathly monotonous at other times. What some called 'cabin fever' could cause a man to do incredibly stupid things, and the wagon trains that had crossed the plains and traversed the mountains sometimes had more trouble from men fighting over women than they did from Indians. Not that the Indians weren't a threat. Pap had fought Apaches and Sioux and considered himself lucky to be alive. In his sixty-seven years he'd experienced everything the west could throw at him, and he'd survived.

Heat waves shimmered above the desert as the figure moved slowly closer. It would be a long hot day with little breeze to cool them. If they were lucky, a breeze would drift down from the mountains at twilight and cool them as the sun sank below the blistering horizon. But now all they knew was this interminable heat.

Pap was comfortable sitting outside of his cantina, shaded by a makeshift overhang that he had overpaid Albert Richards to build years ago. Albert was long dead and the slated overhang was in disrepair, but it was enough. The sun was too damn bright and Pap wore his old cavalry hat to shade his eyes. He squinted into the distance and marked the progress of the man riding in his direction.

A blackbird dropped soundlessly on the ground in front of him and began pecking at the dirt. The damn birds were a nuisance. What the hell was it eating? These damn birds could find something to eat when there was nothing to eat, Pap thought wryly, or maybe they were just waiting to feed on him like a vulture would.

Another blackbird had appeared and the two birds pecked mindlessly at the dirt. Pap had to resist the urge to lift the shotgun propped next to his chair and blow the birds into eternity. The figure in the distance was still indistinguishable, but Pap knew the man well, no matter that seven years had passed.

Down the street he heard shouting and the sound of breaking glass. Three men burst through the batwing doors of the Fool's Gold Saloon. The first man Pap recognized as Michael Keith, the barman at The Fool's Gold. The other two were Sam and Pete Usher and they had Michael bleeding from the mouth.

Hot damn! Pap thought. *The timing couldn't be any better!*

He glanced out at the mirage-like figure simmering in the distance. Then he held his gaze on the three combatants. Sam caught Michael on the jaw with a hard right that spun him around. Pete had danced around and came up behind him, slamming an uppercut into his jaw as he fell backward. Michael flopped to the ground and Sam kicked him in the ribs. Michael howled. Pete spat a wad of mucus into the dust and tried to kick him in the head but Michael covered his head with his hands. Sam and Pete laughed uproariously. Pap could hear them gloating.

'Damn you, boy! You ain't much of a fighting man!'

'You got him beat good, Sam, that you do!'

'I surely think I might shoot him and put him out of his misery!'

'He ain't worth no bullet!'

Pap felt a pang of regret over Michael's plight. It was

7

Sunday and not even noon yet, but everyone in town knew that Sam and Pete Usher liked to get drunk every Sunday morning. This invariably led to unwarranted fights and more than a few killings. Pap kept a sawed-off shotgun at his side just in case the boys ever set their sights on him, but he'd been lucky, they left him alone. Pap had told their old man years ago he wouldn't hesitate to cut them both down without provocation if they gave him the slightest hint of trouble. The old man had glared at him without speaking, but Pap reckoned his message got across all right. They had left him alone. But Pap knew it wasn't fear of his shotgun that kept them at bay. More than likely it was his friendship with the man he believed was now riding back into town that gave the Ushers a moment's pause.

The figure in the distance was still too far away to see clearly but details were beginning to emerge through the wavering heat and shimmering sunlight. He rode a black horse; his hat was tan with a brim pulled low and stained from sweat; he wore a gun on his right hip; a Winchester resided in a saddle boot.

Pap knew that rifle would be loaded. The Colt in his holster would have six in the cylinder because the rider was a man that took no chances. Most gunmen kept the Colt's hammer down on an empty cylinder for safety, but not this man.

Michael Keith pulled himself to his feet. He spat blood and glared at his attackers.

'You sons of bitches don't have the right to push me around. You haven't earned that right!'

Michael's fist was lightning fast and tore a bloody streak across Sam's lips. Then the three of them were close together, slugging it out. The street was filled with the sound of knuckles slamming into bodies. This furious battle eventually paused and Michael tottered between the Usher brothers. He was taking a terrible beating and Pap knew it was only a matter of time before he succumbed to their attack.

He looked out at the blistering desert. The figure in the distance was closer.

Pete lunged forward and kicked Michael's legs out from under him. He plopped unceremoniously to the street in a cloud of dust. Sam and Pete chortled gleefully. Michael moaned in the dirt.

'You got a pretty wife,' Sam said. 'Maybe I'll go pay her a visit.'

'We need some fresh doves in this town,' Pete said.

'His wife will do fine.'

Pete kicked Michael and this set off a flurry of kicking. Michael thrashed on the ground with his arms covering his head but Pap could see that he was taking painful strikes in the ribs. The Usher boys giggled sardonically.

Pap pulled a gold watch from his pocket and scrutinized the timepiece. Eleven thirty-three. Hell, it wasn't even noon yet. His stomach growled. About noon he'd been planning on cooking up some beans and tortillas. Lunch would have to wait. Hell, if they lived through the afternoon that would make dinner all the better.

Michael pulled himself to his feet.

'Well lookie here! He's ain't finished yet!' Sam and Pete watched fearlessly as Michael dusted himself off. His eyes were nearly swollen shut, his face mottled with purple bruises. His lip was split and blood dribbled down his chin.

The rider had reached the outskirts of town, his head

held high, his gaze set on the street where the Usher boys stood glaring at Michael.

Another few moments, Pap thought, just another few moments.

Michael, perhaps sensing the rider, turned his head and squinted at the figure. The Usher boys turned to look as well and Pap studied their expressions. It took them at least a full minute before they recognized him and their features took on an incredulous slant followed by the first hint of fear. The three combatants stared in abject awe as the man on horseback slowly trotted into town. Sam was the first to speak.

'Cole Tibbs?'

The name hung in the air as a question but when Pete repeated the name it had been transformed into a pronouncement that Pap knew would send shockwaves throughout the territory.

'Cole Tibbs. That's him all right.'

The rider came down the street and reined his horse before Pap's cantina. He looked at Pap and frowned.

'You half-breed son of a bitch. I thought they would have killed you by now.'

Pap chuckled. 'Good to see you too. I'm hardly worth their time. And it took you long enough to get back.'

Tibbs nodded. 'I was busy up in Wyoming.'

'I heard about that. You and some marshal named O'Hara took on some cattle rustlers.'

'That we did.' Tibbs looked up the street. The Usher boys hadn't moved, incredulity still carved on their features. 'Looks like Michael's got his hands full.'

'He gave a good account of himself, but the Ushers don't play fair.'

'No, they never did.'

Tibbs held his gaze on the three men and Pap wished he knew what was going through his mind.

Pap's dog Grant rose up and sauntered over to Tibb's horse, his nose sniffing the air. 'You still have this mangy cur.'

'He makes a good watchdog at night. Tibbs, do you want some advice?'

'No.'

'I didn't think so, but I'll offer it anyway just so I can sleep good at night knowing I did the right thing. Get out of town before they kill you.'

Tibbs chuckled. It was a slow, good-hearted laugh that almost convinced Pap that Tibbs could handle anything that came his way.

'I thought I'd stick around awhile.' Tibbs glanced down at the shotgun. 'Keep that thing handy. You have any other guns?'

'Got a derringer in my pocket I won off a whore in a poker game.'

'The old man around?'

'Not much, but I reckon you'll have your hands full no matter what.'

'And Les and Edgar?'

'They run the place pretty much now. They're out of town right now on business. The old man hasn't been well.'

Tibbs didn't like hearing that Les and Edgar were out of town. He would have to make certain they returned, and soon. He returned his gaze to the Usher boys. Michael caught Tibbs's eye and nodded. A thin smile stretched across Michael's battered face.

11

'I reckon I better get this done.'

Tibbs gave the reins a tug and he cantered down the street. The blackbirds pecking at the dust hopped irritably out his way as his horse closed the distance on the Usher boys. He came up close and turned his horse to face them. Michael slowly moved off to his right. Tibbs nodded at Michael again.

'Michael, good to see you. I hope your wife and family are well.'

'They are. You're looking good, Tibbs. I heard you had some excitement up in Wyoming.'

'Nothing to it,' Tibbs said.

'I never thought you would show your face around these parts again.' It was Sam who had spoken and as he said the words he appraised Tibbs with contempt, a sneer on his lips. Tibbs returned the stare. His features were calm and he gave an outward appearance of confidence.

'Last time you were here you was too drunk to do much of anything,' Pete said.

'That's a fact,' Tibbs said. 'Now I have some unfinished business to settle with Sam here.'

'You ain't got no business with me,' Sam said. 'But if you'd like to get off that horse I'll give you a good beating just like last time.' At this the Usher brothers laughed wickedly as if this were the best comedic line they'd ever uttered.

Tibbs nodded. 'I suppose you'd like that.' With lightning speed Tibbs had his Colt in his hand with the hammer back. And just as quickly he sighted down the barrel and shot Pete in the leg. The gunshot echoed loudly against the storefronts and the blackbirds cawed uneasily and ruffled their feathers. Pete crumpled with his

12

hands plastered to his wound, blood bursting from the hole. He howled in pain. Tibbs leveled his Colt on Sam.

'Michael, if you could remove Pete's gunbelt I'd appreciate it.'

Michael tore Pete's gunbelt free.

'Now drop it in that horse trough if you would be so kind.'

With Pete's gunbelt rusting at the bottom of the horse trough, Michael looked at Tibbs and said, 'I'm glad you're back, Tibbs, but I wouldn't give odds on you living long.'

'We'll see about that. Give my best to your wife.'

'I'll do that.'

Pap, having risen from his chair to observe the showdown up close, waited until Michael had returned to The Fool's Gold Saloon before he advanced on the scene. Tension hung in the air thicker than the heatwave that turned the desert yellow and a man's shirt wet with perspiration. Pap wanted a cool drink right then. Maybe a tall glass of whiskey with ice, except there was no ice in Raven Flats. He wondered if Tibbs wanted a glass of whiskey as well.

'Now Pete, you'll be certain to tell your father what transpired here today.'

Pete, rasping through clenched teeth, said, 'You're damn right I'll tell him! And Sam and I will hunt you down, you bastard! You had no right to shoot me!'

'Yes I did. Now Sam please slowly pull your gun from its holster.'

Sam, incredulous and mute with amazement at the scene unfolding around him, eased his Colt from its holster. He held it loosely in his hand and down alongside his leg.

13

'Good boy. You're just like a well-trained dog. Pete, don't forget to tell your old man what I said here. I said that Sam is like a well-trained dog.'

'Damn you to hell!' Pete hissed.

'Sam, do you recall that you killed my father?'

Sam's eyes blazed with fury. 'I remember all right. That old coot had it coming. Anyone that crosses the Ushers is gonna get what's due them!'

'That may be true,' Tibbs said, 'But you killed an unarmed man and then beat me bloody when I was drunk. There's also the matter of the Tibbs homestead now being occupied by your family.'

'You have nowhere to go. That property is ours now. You best leave before you get yourself killed. My pa ain't gonna be happy to hear that you're back.'

'Sam, you need to lift that gun and point it at me. You might get lucky and kill me before I kill you.'

Sam's eyes widened in shock. 'What?!'

Tibbs shook his head as if he were scolding a naughty boy. He looked off at the desert and its many heat mirages dancing like ghosts on the horizon, and then back at Sam.

'This is your only chance. Shoot me, you dumb son of a bitch!'

Slowly the awareness of his situation dawned on Sam. There was a moment when his face was shadowed by a glimmer of fear, but as Tibbs had expected, his demeanor quickly changed to defiance. His hand came up, and quickly. Pap would long recall the sound of the hammer being pulled back and the glint of haughty arrogance in Sam's eyes as Tibbs blew a hole through his chest. His gun spewed flame and blue smoke, the slug crashing through Sam's breastbone and disintegrating his spine as it exited

14

out of his back followed by a fountain of blood. He was dead before he hit the ground; his eyes rolled back in their sockets as he slammed into the dusty street. His body twitched convulsively but in a moment he lay still.

The scene would be etched in Pap's mind forever – Sam's lifeless body in the dust; the smoke curling from the Colt's muzzle as Tibbs slid it back into his holster; Pete screaming on the ground, 'You murdering bastard! You can't get away with this! My pa's gonna hunt you down, Tibbs! Do you hear me? You're a dead man. . . !' And the blackbirds in the street went about their business pecking at scraps of offal.

Tibbs slid out of his saddle and grabbed the bridle. Without looking back he led his horse down the street and lashed the reins to a hitching post. He followed Pap into his cantina. The room was windowless, cool, the long bar no more than several planks propped between two barrels. There were two empty tables and an overturned chair in the corner.

'How's business?' Tibbs asked sarcastically.

'Pedro and a few Mexican boys come in once a month. You want a glass of whiskey?'

Pap slid behind the bar and pulled up a brown bottle.

'Nope,' Tibbs said. 'I only drink whiskey twice a year. One on my birthday and one on Christmas day.'

Pap raised an eyebrow. 'I'll be damned. Well, we've all heard stories about you. I guess you're not the drunk they chased out of town.'

'You have any coffee?' Tibbs asked.

'I have a can of Arbuckles. I'll make us both some.'

Pap shuffled into the back room and Tibbs once again studied his surroundings. The cantina hadn't changed at all. Tibbs would have sworn the same cobwebs clung to the low-ceiling corners. He kept an eye on the doorway, the sun shimmering out in the street like a cauldron. He could hear Pete Usher caterwauling like a damn fool down the street. He estimated he had till sundown – Usher's men would make their first strike just as the sun was dropping below the mountains. It would be cooler then. He reminded himself he couldn't afford any mistakes. These men were all cold, ruthless killers. If he was to succeed he would have to be equally cold and ruthless. He had shown them today that he was ready.

Pap returned with two cups of coffee. He sat on a stool behind the bar and faced Tibbs. 'Where do you plan on sleeping? The hotel won't give you a room. Usher owns it. He owns damn near this entire town. You can sleep in my backroom but I wouldn't bet either one of us would live through the night. Now what have you got going for you?'

Tibbs raised an eyebrow and pulled his Colt from his holster. 'This gun was custom made by the Colt Manufacturing Company to my specifications. It has a hair trigger and the hammer pulls back as easy as spreading butter. I use it only in self-defense and I rarely miss.'

'Looks to be a seven inch barrel.'

'Seven and a half inches to be exact.'

'And you got a rifle in your saddle boot on the horse.'

'A '73 model Winchester. I had the lever customized by a gunsmith in Denver.'

Pap chuckled and sipped his coffee. 'Yesiree, I guess you got it all figured out. But even if you are fast with a gun you're gonna be outnumbered.'

Now it was Tibbs's turn to chuckle. He tapped his fore-

16

finger to his head. 'Planning, Paps. Planning is every-thing.'

'So what's the plan?'

Tibbs frowned. 'The less you know the better off you'll be.'

'You gone loco? You better have a plan that works or you'll be dead by sundown!'

'I have one. I'm going to kill each and every one of those Usher boys and then I'm going to kill the old man.'

Pap was taken aback by the harsh tone and chilling words.

'But, Cole, you can't just gun them down. Now today you have witnesses that Sam pulled a gun on you, but you goaded him. How exactly do you plan on doing this and not breaking the law?'

Tibbs narrowed his eyes, his lips tight. Finally he said, 'Make no mistake about it. I've had seven long years to think this over. I promise you that every man I kill will have a gun in his hand.'

CHAPTER TWO

Carleton Usher lived in a sprawling ranch house populated by shadows and dreamed of corpses. The many windows were covered with large damask drapery, the rooms lit by oil lamps that threw shadows across the walls even in daylight. He shunned the sunlight. He stood with his back to the wall and smoked a cigar, the gray smoke curling about his head like an angry ghost.

It would be remarked later that if he had known of the anguish he was about to experience he might have repented. He might have thrown his arms heavenward and asked God forgiveness for his many sins, for Carleton Usher was a man responsible for many deaths, and while they haunted him, he reveled in his victories all the same.

He had spent the morning going over his business ledgers at his desk when he dozed off and dreamed about the Union soldiers charging over the ridge. The sound of the muskets volleyed in his mind and he moaned, drool spilling from his open mouth as he turned his head, blinked his eyes, and woke up. A corpse had been rushing toward him, the hollow eyes of the dead accusing him.

He forced himself to his feet. He wiped the spittle from

18

his chin, lit a cigar and stood with his back to the wall. He didn't enjoy the fact that he was getting old. Only an old man fell asleep at his desk and suffered nightmares of the past, he thought.

He crossed the room and examined himself in the mirror. The man that stared back at him was not pleasant looking. If anything, his features might be described as reptilian. The cold, brown eyes were set deep into the sockets of his aquiline face, his hair, while plentiful, was pure white. Years of exposure to the southwestern sunlight had turned his skin into something akin to wrinkled parchment. His crooked, but razor thin nose reminded people of a buzzard's profile. Tall and gaunt, he favored black clothing and strangers to Raven Flats often mistook him for an undertaker.

These facts were all well known to Carleton Usher, but they had no effect on his disposition. Usher was a man that had long ago come to grips with his ugliness, and so he compensated by flaunting his power. Wealth had bought him that power. And while no sane woman would willingly consort with him, his sons were bought and paid for by women so desperate for money they would have been kind to Satan himself. Love was unknown to him. His passion was money and power.

During the war he had fought against the Union scum that had destroyed his father's plantation. How he hated those blue belly Yankees to this day. If he had ever experienced true happiness it came on the battlefield when he ran his bayonet into a bluecoat. He killed his first man in 1862 – he had killed many men since then. But his dreams of the war had not ceased in twenty years. He could recall with remarkable clarity the features of every man he had killed since.

He returned to his desk and finished reviewing his business ledgers. As he was closing the book he heard the church bells ringing across the desert. It was noon in Raven Flats. No doubt Sam and Pete were tangled up with some soiled doves by now. Those boys spent more time whoring and drinking than any of his sons.

He strode from the room and found Conchita, his housemaid. Ordering her to bring him lunch in his den, he returned to his desk where he smoked another cigar and leafed through the pages of a book by James Fenimore Cooper. He considered reading but a modest pleasure. He was often disappointed that the characters were never as strong as he fancied himself. So high was Usher's opinion of himself that he once wrote to a dime magazine publisher and complained that none of the stories featured a protagonist with the practical if not ruthless business acumen that made Usher feared throughout the southwest territory. The publisher never replied.

Presently Conchita brought him some chicken, potatoes, and scrambled eggs. He wolfed down his food and drank half a glass of bourbon. Rather than smoke another cigar he rolled himself a cigarette on a thin square of paper using a sprinkling of tobacco from a pouch. The room was heady with smoke, the scent of food and Usher's body odor.

He had finished the cigarette when there was a knock at the door. Usher entertained few visitors and so the interruption surprised him.

'Come in!' he barked.

One of his *vaqueros*, Feliciano, stood nervously in the doorway.

'What is it? Don't stand there like a fool. Say your piece!'

Feliciano held his sombrero in his hands, twisting its brim between his fingers.

'Señor, your son . . . he has . . . you come see . . . a man with a gun. . . .'

Feliciano, clearly fearing Usher's wrath, bowed his head. Usher, perplexed, sprang from his chair.

'Show me.'

He followed Feliciano out of the room and on to the porch. Another *vaquero*, Franco, was climbing from the buckboard. Pete was in the rear, his face ashen.

'What in tarnation happened?' Usher bellowed.

'Pa! Sam's dead! He was shot by Cole Tibbs! Pa, I'm hurt bad!'

Usher could scarcely believe what he was hearing. He went up to the buckboard, leaned over and looked down at Sam's body. Sam's lifeless eyes reflected the fierce molten sun.

'I'll be damned. He's as dead as Julius Caesar.'

For Feliciano, observing this from the porch, Usher's reaction was no surprise. There was no emotion other than an almost casual surprise at seeing his son's corpse.

He set his gaze on Pete. 'Tell me what happened.'

Feliciano and Franco both knew it was a command. And they knew what would come next. So Pete told his father what happened, and in his version of events Tibbs had surprised them before they could draw their guns. It was nearly true. When he was finished his father said to Franco. 'Get the whelp a doctor.'

Feliciano was prepared. He had known coming in from town how this would play out. He said a silent prayer for

Cole Tibbs. Usher held his gaze and said 'Go send a telegram to Les and Edgar in Colorado, then round up the boys. Take twelve men into town and bring Tibbs to me alive or kill him if you have to. Alive is preferable only because I'd enjoy killing him myself, but such a Yankee dog may prove troublesome and you'll be forced to kill him. Do you understand?'

'Yes, *señor.*'

'Go.'

So Feliciano went from the ranch with a heavy heart, but he would follow his instructions diligently. To disobey Usher meant certain death. He paused briefly at the bunkhouse and spoke to José. Then he went to the stables and saddled his horse. Maria and Conchita appeared in the doorway to observe him. He spoke briefly to them as well and watched as they returned to the house.

When his horse was saddled he went to the second bunkhouse where the gringo ranch-hands all slept. Bret Hagard, the foreman, sat at a table playing cards with three other men. Feliciano told Hagard what happened and what was expected. Hagard's eyes widened. 'Well, I'll be damned. Shooting that Tibbs boy will be a sight more interesting than playing cards.' He pushed back his chair and strode from the room. After a moment all of the *gringos* – eight in all – strapped on their gunbelts and followed him.

Feliciano returned to the stables and mounted his horse. He rode away from the ranch without glancing back. For Feliciano knew that his survival depended on his carrying out his task perfunctorily. Like Usher, he would conduct his business efficiently and without emotion. An image of Sam Usher's lifeless eyes flashed through his mind and he thought of the old man looking down on the corpse without grief. Such a cold, hard man, perhaps in some ways like a dead man himself. Feliciano knew the loss of his son was only the equivalent of a business loss for a man like Usher.

The Usher ranch was three miles from Raven Flats. Feliciano rode across a sandy stretch of land and into the hills that formed a natural barrier between the town and the ranch. The land was rich with ocotillo shrub, manzanita brush, and juniper trees. He passed a long stretch of prickly pear cactus and then crossed a swell of small hills and into a swale of tall, desert grass to a place they called Snakebite Creek. The creek ran down from the mountains and created the last boundary to Usher's property before the earth gave way to more desert.

Feliciano remembered what had happened there seven years before and again had to force his memories aside. This was no time for reflection. He could reflect later, in church, and ask God forgiveness. All the same, a chill ran down his spine as he crossed Snakebite Creek. Along the creek the tall grass and cattails swayed in the hot sun. His horse clopped out of the water and into the grass and Feliciano reined up as he heard the telltale rattle.

The warm breeze suddenly vanished like a cat slinking into the distance. The air hung like an invisible curtain, smothering, thick, hot.

Sweat began to drip down from beneath his sombrero. His eyes struck at the grass seeking any slithering sign of the rattlesnakes that ruled this ungodly dominion. His saw the slow curl of a fat rattler three feet on his left. Down on his right another rattler slithered deeper into the grass. The sound of rattlers filled the air like a frightening chant. He peered ahead, judging the best route for his horse.

The thin, barren trail through the grass and past the gleaming rocks told of a thousand departures from Snakebite Creek. He whispered a prayer. Of course, it would have been easier to circumnavigate the creek and come around from the west where he could have crossed the creek at a place bereft of rattlers, but such was the urgency to follow Usher's instructions that he chose to put himself at risk. Feliciano feared Usher more than he feared the snakes.

He dug his spurs into his horse and pressed on. If he stayed off the rocks and out of the tall grass there would be less chance his horse would encounter a snake. The animal trail they followed was known to but a few. When he was out of the grass the trail rose into the rocks that formed a natural barrier and it was here that the rattlers lazed on the rocks sunning themselves. He rode out of the rocks and down on to the desert again, the sound of rattlers fading behind him.

Raven Flats glimmered in the distance. Within the hour the *gringos* would come led by Hagard. Then José and Ramón would follow. Twelve of them in all to kill one man. Twelve men like the *gringos* had on a jury. Except this was Usher's game and there was nothing fair about it. Feliciano crossed himself.

It was two-thirty in the afternoon when Feliciano finished sending the telegram. Now Edgar and Les would come, and they would mourn their brother. He left the telegraph office and looked up and down the street. The boardwalk was empty; a few blackbirds were scattered in the street pecking at crumbs. The shade beneath the overhang outside of Pap Wingfoot's cantina was inviting but empty. He wondered if Tibbs had gone inside with the old

24

man. He decided to look for his horse. Ten minutes later he found it inside the livery.

'You talk to the man?' he asked Chaco, the stable hand. Chaco nodded and spoke rapidly in Spanish. The man had come an hour ago and then taken his rifle and saddle-bags and walked away. Chaco had remained with the horse. He hadn't wished to know which direction the man had gone. Feliciano thanked him and left.

He walked past the blackbirds that cawed in the street as they pecked at the dust. His spurs jangled as he followed the boardwalk to Pap Wingfoot's cantina.

'Hello, *señor.*'

'Come in slow,' Pap grumbled from the dark interior.

Feliciano pushed past the batwing doors and stopped. It took a moment for his eyes to adjust to the gloom.

'That's close enough,' Pap said.

'*Señor,* they will come soon. I have to see that he is not here.'

'He's not, so you can tell the truth.'

Feliciano nodded. Pap was sitting behind the bar, his shotgun resting across the plank table.

'*Señor,* this boy Tibbs will die. He must run.'

'He's not a boy any longer and he won't run. But I suspect you're right about him dying. The only question I have is how many of Usher's men will he take with him.'

Feliciano's mouth was dry and he had a difficult time swallowing.

'Now you're a smart Mexican.' Pap continued. 'And I know you don't have a stomach for killing. My advice to you is don't give Tibbs a reason to aim his hogleg at you.'

Again, Feliciano nodded. 'Yes, *señor,* I thought of that. *Vaya con dios.*'

He backed out of the cantina slowly and breathed a sigh of relief when he once again felt the hot sun on his back. The old man was just as dangerous as Usher and Feliciano knew that his shotgun had a hair trigger.

He walked slowly up the street and sat in a chair on the boardwalk outside of the telegraph office. An interminable length of time passed. Hagard wasn't in a hurry. The boys would undoubtedly take a few snorts of whiskey before saddling their horses. The blackbirds in the street had taken wing and settled on the telegraph wire. They perched like dark sentries awaiting a day of reckoning. A shiver ran down Feliciano's spine.

He wondered what kind of man Cole Tibbs had become. What kind of man comes to his death alone? Pap wouldn't be much help. Tibbs was hopelessly outnumbered. Feliciano discovered that he was eager to see Tibbs again. The boy that had been beaten and chased from town must be quite a man now, or the biggest fool. And he sensed that Tibbs was no fool.

Thirty minutes later Hagard rode into town followed by the other ranch-hands. They were all armed with Colt revolvers. José and Ramón followed close behind. Hagard spurred his horse and came up to the boardwalk to glower at Feliciano.

'Where is he?' Hagard demanded.

'I do not know, *señor*. His horse is in the stable. The old man sits in his cantina with a shotgun.'

Hagard glanced about. 'I reckon he's hiding then.' He waved an arm at the men. 'Dismount and look for him. Let's get this done quick so I can have another drink.'

And so the first search began. In an hour they had searched every building. Hagard himself entered Pap's cantina to question him but emerged scowling. 'No sign of him. If that old man knows anything I'll kill him later.'

And so the second search began. 'Check every room and every attic and cellar!' Hagard growled. 'I want that bastard found!'

This time their search was meticulous. Against the protests of many they entered every home and searched every room. They peered into cellars and attics, outhouses and storage sheds. They shoved pitchforks into bales of hay. They swept aside dust balls and raccoons' nests and found nothing.

Pap Wingfoot emerged from his cantina and once again sat on his chair under the awning, the shotgun balanced across his knees. Hagard approached him again.

'If I found out you've been hiding him I'll kill you.'

'See for yourself,' Pap said.

Hagard took four men and searched every corner of Pap's cantina. Hagard came out with his face flushed.

'Where do you reckon he went, old timer?'

Pap spit a wad of chewing tobacco into the dust. 'I have no idea. But I'll tell you this. You chased a drunk boy out of town seven years ago. Now a man has come back with a gun. It's only been a few hours and one of Usher's boys is dead. What does that tell you about the man you're searching for?'

Feliciano listened to this with interest. Tibbs had disappeared. Indeed, where had the *gringo* gone? He looked out at the parched, whispering desert sand in that long stretch between Raven Flats and the Usher ranch. The uncaring desert was filled with arroyos of silence and shimmering mirages that danced like unholy ghosts. And the only sound in that dangerous no-man's-land was the distant rattle of snakes shifting uneasily across the rocks and the hollow cawing of the blackbirds on the telegraph wire.

CHAPTER THREE

If Conchita had looked up from her washbasin at three o'clock that afternoon she would have seen a figure racing between the sagebrush on the northwest perimeter. She might have recognized Cole Tibbs as the young man the girls fancied all those years ago, but Tibbs had been deemed an unworthy suitor – he was lazy and drunk most of the time. If Conchita could have looked closely into his eyes as he raced across the sand she would have seen a steely glint in his eyes and a fierce intelligence that would have given her a moment's pause, for this was the same man in body only. The heart and mind of Cole Tibbs was something new. But Conchita was busy washing clothes and failed to look up as Tibbs disappeared behind the barn.

Tibbs, of course, had seen Conchita and chose to keep his presence a secret. He wouldn't take a chance that she might raise the alarm even though she had no quarrel with him. The Mexicans had never fought against him but Usher paid well for their loyalty. Tibbs crept along the barn and paused at the corner, his heart pulsing madly. He would allow himself twenty minutes to accomplish his goal. He slipped a gold watch from his vest pocket and checked the time. Slipping the watch back into his pocket he made for the house.

He came up along the side porch and slipped into the kitchen. From here he made his way quickly through a drawing room until he came to a door. He brushed aside memories of happier times when his family still lived. He listened at the door. Yes. . . .

Carleton Usher looked up from his desk as the door suddenly opened and Cole Tibbs walked into the room. He was astounded. Tibbs stood calmly if not brazenly before him. His demeanor bespoke confidence. He had not drawn his gun, his arms hung loosely at his sides, but the man's eyes told of his lethal abilities. Usher shuddered.

'You bastard!' he nearly spat the words.

'Keep your hands on the desk,' Tibbs said.

'What are you doing here? My men will return at any moment. I'll have you run out of town yet again!' But Usher's voice was feeble and Tibbs frowned.

'I'm here to give you one chance to save your life.'

'That's preposterous! I haven't broken any laws! You can't come bursting in here and threaten me!'

'You have broken some laws and we both know your money has kept you away from the hangman's noose.'

'Get out of this house this instant!'

Tibbs stepped forward and leveled his gaze on Usher. The old man shivered at the determination and self-confidence that shone from those eyes.

'This is what I want you to do,' Tibbs said. 'I want you to sign over all of your property to me. I want you to return to me all that you have stolen. For this I'll let you live. To

30

refuse will mean your death.'

Usher was enraged. He slapped his palm on the desk. 'This is an outrage! You killed my son and now you want my home! I'll see you hang, Tibbs!'

And again Usher saw the self-confidence and lack of fear in the man's face.

'I'm not surprised,' Tibbs said. 'I never thought you would do the right thing, but I had to try.'

'By God, you're a fool! And your father was a fool before you!'

Tibbs was silent a moment. Finally he said, 'Yes, I think he was. He was foolish to enter into a business arrangement with a man like you, and I was equally the fool by spending my time drinking whiskey and playing cards.'

'My sons should have killed you when they had the chance!'

'Such harsh words.' Tibbs paused. He appeared to be studying Usher. The man was thin and frail. The wrinkles beneath his eyes clung to his face like cobwebs. Even in the stifling confines of the curtained room he wore a dark wool dovetailed coat. Tibbs thought the man looked like an undertaker. The oil lamps cast Usher's shadow on the wall like a grotesque parody of the man himself. In any other circumstances Tibbs would have pitied the man, but then he recalled his father and his voice was as unrelenting as a cold wind when he next spoke. 'I'm going to take everything away from you,' Tibbs continued. 'Before this is over you'll beg for mercy. I suggest you contact Les and Edgar and get them back here. I'd like a few words with them.' Tibbs let his gaze sweep around the room taking in the curtained windows and the flickering shadows cast by the oil lamps. The house had become like a tomb.

31

'What business could you have with my sons? They'll kill you on sight!'

'Just get them here.'

Tibbs smiled thinly and backed toward the door, his eyes never leaving Usher. He stopped at the door and gave a resigned shrug before slipping from the house.

The sunlight was a relief after the stifling confines of Usher's den. Tibbs followed a route behind the barn and once again observed Conchita at her washbasin. He would have to be fast now. Usher's men would have completed their search of the town and would be making their way back to the ranch. He checked his pocket watch and when Conchita had her back to him he raced for a patch of cactus that would provide cover.

The path he followed led him straight to Snakebite Creek. Unlike most he was wary but unafraid of the pre-ponderance of rattlesnakes that made this area their home. He entered the grassy area that bordered the creek and then stepped off the trail on to the rocks. This section of rocky terrain formed a swell that ran three hundred yards on both sides of the creek. It was impossible for horses to get their footing here and travelers between the ranch and town would keep to the trail. Tibbs saw several snakes coiled on the rocks, the faint murmur of their rattles whispering a warning. But he moved swiftly and silently, keeping wide of any direct contact with the snakes.

There was an indentation in the rocks about forty feet long and it was here that he had left his rifle, canteen, and saddle-bags. When crouched he was invisible to travelers. He could peer over the ridge on either side and mark any movement in that sandy stretch leading to the ranch or the town opposite. His saddle-bag was heavy with beef jerky and cartridges. Tibbs estimated he could hide here for three days and survive.

He removed his Stetson and wiped the sweat from his face with his bandanna. The sun was making slow progress as it dipped toward the horizon. He would rest but a few hours before embarking upon the next stage of his plan. He unholstered his gun, punched out the two spent cartridges, and replaced them. Not long after, he heard muffled voices and the clip-clop of hoofbeats. Carefully slinking up the rock he glanced out at Raven Flats. As expected, riders were heading toward the Usher ranch. With their search complete a contingent was being sent back to Usher. There would be hell to pay when they learned Tibbs had confronted the old man. It was looking to be a busy night.

Tibbs hunkered down and waited, his senses alert as the riders crossed the creek and brushed slowly through the tall grass. Wary of rattlers, their voices died down as they skirted the rocks not forty feet from Tibbs. When they had passed, they resumed their canter and drifted toward the ranch. Now Tibbs expected to find out if he had chosen the right location.

An hour passed and the sun dropped closer to the horizon. Tibbs drank a swallow from his canteen and ate some beef jerky. Another thirty minutes passed and the shadows began to lengthen. Finally the sky paled and the amber shadows pooled into silhouettes that flung themselves across the rocks like mourners.

For many the desert is a desolate place, empty and forbidding. But Tibbs thought of the desert as a living thing. He had spent his life here until they had driven him out, and for him the desert was at once unconquerable and bristling with life. Every juniper tree or thorny patch of mesquite harbored insects, rodents, snakes or Gila monsters. There were places just inches beneath the hot, whispering sand where a knowledgeable man might find water. Tibbs knew the desert and respected its power. He was relying on that knowledge to keep him alive.

With the sun melting below the distant range the desert was bathed in a blue mist that deepened into an amber twilight. There was still enough light to see clearly and he eventually heard another clip-clop chorus on the trail from Usher's ranch. He spied several riders moving in his direction, but not that many. Usher was predictable: he had kept a few men at the ranch and sent a few more, presumably to join Hagard in town.

He slipped down into the crevice as they splashed across the creek. With the sun down there was less chance of snakes on the rocky trail, but Tibbs knew a snake might cross the horse path at any hour. The riders slowed and made their way meticulously across and away from Snakebite Creek. Tibbs wasted no time. He was up and moving across the rocks. He circled the swell of hills and came at the trail from a ninety degree angle as the riders spurred their horses into a gallop. He had the Winchester in his hand as he followed with long strides. It would take him just about an hour to cross two miles of desert. By then the riders would be in town. With Tibbs missing, their likely location would be the Fool's Gold Saloon. Michael Keith was about to have his hands full with a crowd of angry Usher cowhands.

A line of prickly pear cactus barred his way and he circled around, his senses tuned into every sound. The first mile was uneventful. He could see the lights blazing in a few shacks and outlying buildings in Raven Flats. As twilight turned to early evening the town huddled at the horizon. From a distance Raven Flats appeared as a group of square, dark shapes, but as he moved closer Tibbs could discern details. The hotel was lit up and there was a glow emitting from the Fool's Gold Saloon. Voices drifted into the darkening sky. There was a horse near an outhouse at the town's perimeter. One of the riders had stayed behind.

Tibbs blended into the darkness that pooled around a Joshua tree. He propped the Winchester against the tree. The pungent smell of the bell-shaped yucca plant tugged at his senses. He lay flat on the sand and crawled past the yucca plant until he was twenty feet from the outhouse. The scent of the yucca plant was replaced by the scent of the outhouse.

Now he waited. Waiting was something he had practiced for seven years. The sentry was a heavy man, possibly in his mid-thirties. Tibbs didn't recognize him. Drifters came and went on the Usher ranch and in seven years a great many of the men Tibbs had known would have ridden on, if they had lived. All except Hagard.

This one would be easy. He had his back to Tibbs as he smoked a cigarette. Tibbs decided not to kill him. He stood up and steadied his breathing. The night was quiet and warm.

Tibbs said: 'Hello.'

Startled, the man turned, his hand dropping to his gun and Tibbs hit him. His fist broke the man's nose with a *crack!* Then Tibbs brought an uppercut into his sternum and knocked the wind out of him. The man went to his knees gasping for air. Before the man could begin bellowing, Tibbs stepped in and grabbed his wrist. Twisting his palm he turned the man's forearm clockwise and then brought his fist down hard on the man's arm, extending it and breaking it just as the chinamen boxers had taught him in San Francisco that first year after being run out of Raven Flats.

The man began to squeal with pain and Tibbs kicked him in the head. The impact sent him sprawling. Without a second thought Tibbs left the unconscious man in the sand and retrieved his rifle.

He moved easily into town. He studied the street and watched for any additional sentries. He followed an alley behind the Fool's Gold Saloon and stopped. There was an outhouse behind the saloon and a refuse barrel, which stank of rotting food. Another barrel was filled to the brim with empty whiskey bottles. The Fool's Gold Saloon was a two story building and golden light shone through the thin window curtains above him. He heard the sound of a woman giggling. The back entrance led to a storage room. No doubt they had searched it already, so Tibbs slipped in.

He stood in the room a moment and listened. He heard Hagard's voice. Tibbs cracked open the interior door. He could see into the rear of the saloon. Hagard and six men were at a table playing cards and drinking whiskey. Michael Keith was behind the bar. His face was bruised and his lip swollen from the beating he had taken from Sam and Pete Usher. But so far he didn't appear to have additional injuries. Tibbs knew Mike had a shotgun behind the bar. There were other patrons in the bar but none of them were Usher's men.

It was still early. Tibbs decided to wait before he made

his move. He wanted a better feel for the men Usher had sent to kill him. He knew enough about Hagard, and the men at Hagard's table looked predictable enough. They were all guns for hire, no better than Hagard. But he wasn't certain yet about the Mexicans.

Wasting no further time he left the alley, noting the placement of shadows and patches of light. He was swallowed by the darkness and any sentries watching the street would have seen only a shadow moving among the pools of blackness as Tibbs made his way across town. He paused near Pap's cantina to listen. There was a flickering oil lamp inside but no sound. He moved toward the cattle pens, following the railroad tracks.

He found the two Mexican sentries easily enough. They were standing together near the foreman's office, their cigarettes glowing in the dark – they weren't making a good effort at remaining hidden. Tibbs thought about it and then stepped out of the darkness. He followed a fence line until he was twenty feet from the two men. He knew they saw him but they hadn't called out or drawn their guns.

'*Amigo*, it is very dangerous to be outside tonight.' Tibbs recognized Feliciano's voice. The two Mexicans stepped forward. Feliciano and a young kid named José. Tibbs remembered them as decent, hardworking men.

'Are you going to draw those guns?'

'Yes, *señor*. But my aim is not so good. I am growing old and my eyes are bad. You should run now.'

'What about the others?'

'José here cannot shoot well. Ramón is tired tonight. He sleeps over near the train depot. Perhaps if he is startled he will shoot at shadows.'

'How many men does Hagard have with him?'

'Twelve to begin, but I think more riders came. *Señor*, fifty men work for the old man. You cannot win.'

'We'll see about that.'

'I will pray at your grave. This is all I can do.'

'I appreciate that,' Tibbs said. With nothing more to say he turned and walked away. Feliciano had made it clear the Mexicans meant him no harm, but the odds were still against him.

He was fifty feet away and about to turn the corner when Feliciano and José began firing. Tibbs turned and watched them empty their revolvers into the wall of darkness beyond the corral. Tibbs smiled to himself. He knew they would tell a good story about their encounter with Tibbs who somehow managed to escape into the darkness. Then Tibbs was moving fast, cutting across the street as Hagard emerged from the Fool's Gold Saloon. Hagard had two men with him and they raced off toward the stockyards to investigate the gunfire.

Tibbs waited, letting them pass. He wasn't after Hagard tonight. When they were out of sight he backtracked to the rear entrance of the Fool's Gold Saloon. Propping his rifle against the wall he slipped into the doorway and crept to the adjoining door where he glanced out at the card tables. Four men remained, and three others that he thought were residents.

Tibbs was confident when he strode into the room, his arms at his sides. His eyes never wavered from the four men. They looked up in astonishment.

'Who are you?' one man said. The four men were too startled to move but their hands dropped near their holsters.

Tibbs frowned. 'Boys, you can surrender now. All that's required is that you leave your guns on the table and saddle up and ride on. I reckon that's your best bet tonight.'

The men snorted and chuckled.

'You're Tibbs ain't you?'

'Are you going to surrender or not?'

The men looked at each other with amusement. Their own confidence was growing.

'Mister, you must be damn loco. There's four guns here. Not even old Wild Bill was fast enough to draw on four men.'

Tibbs laughed. It was a hearty, sincere chortle that flew from his lips. 'That's right boys, I guess Wild Bill learned his lesson in Deadwood. But I'm not Wild Bill.'

'Tibbs.'

'Let's get the dance going if that's your preference.'

The men rose, pushing chairs back, the wood creaking, boots scuffling the hardwood floor as they heaved to their feet. One man had his gun drawn before he was out of his chair and Tibbs shot him in the chest. The detonation echoed like a thunderclap and a moment of pandemonium ensued. With his right finger holding the trigger in place, Tibbs fanned his left hand over the hammer in a technique few gunfighters could master with such speed. The Colt barked, spewing flame and blue smoke. Crimson flowers bloomed across plaid shirts and snarls changed to pallid looks of astonishment as bodies tumbled, overturning the table. The room filled with the roar of the gun and the crash of splintered wood as all four men tumbled to their deaths, their guns clutched uselessly in their hands.

From behind the bar Michael Keith said, 'You're full of surprises.'

Tibbs punched out the spent shells and replaced the cartridges. He holstered his gun and said, 'Mike, tell Hagard I'm coming for him. I want him to think about that, and that I'm taking my time coming after him.'

'I'll do that.'

Tibbs turned and walked out of the saloon, picked up his rifle and made his way along the dark alley. His stride was purposeful but not hurried. The gunshots still echoed in his ears as he made his way across the desert trail, past the stretch of prickly pear cactus and yucca plants. The night was still and warm.

Finally he circled away from the trail, brushing out his boot prints with a branch. He came upon Snakebite Creek and paused, listening for sounds. Nothing. As expected, he was alone. Tibbs heard only the whisper of the creek. He climbed into the rocks and settled into his hiding place. He set his rifle aside and unbuckled his gunbelt. He took the Colt from the holster and lay down with his saddle-bags as a pillow. Tibbs was neither hungry nor fatigued, but he knew he had to rest.

With the Colt in his hand he willed his body to relax. He had been in town but one day and he knew that surviving the next forty-eight hours would be a greater challenge. But he had planned well, after all. His hand went to his vest pocket, his fingers tracing the object he held there in secret. The metal was cold and sharp.

Hagard and the other men would be frightened now, and desperate. In a few days Les and Edgar Usher would arrive on the train. And one other man. That third passenger would be vital in securing peace in Raven Flats.

40

Tibbs pulled the tin star from his vest and scrutinized it in the starlight, for his was not a vendetta alone, but the mission of a deputy US marshal.

CHAPTER FOUR

For the old Mexicans the desert was a place where the eternal struggle of life over death was enacted in a rich tableau across the swells of sand and soil and mesquite. Its breathtaking beauty was as wondrous and as deceptive as a harlot's body. The cruel land bristled with lethal traps for it was here that the scorpion and spider, the rattler and coyote claimed the land as their own. Of men only the Apache had perfected their ability to survive in such a harsh and uncompromising landscape. And now the Apache was beaten, not by the desert, but by the white men who came to forge crossroad towns like Raven Flats. Morning broke over the southwest with a golden light that painted the far mountains as a purple haze and rendered the desert and scrubland surrounding Raven Flats as a lonely land of Joshua trees and swells of baked sand or blistering rocks.

Cole Tibbs sat hunched between two barrels in the alley behind the Fool's Gold Saloon. His Stetson was pulled low over his eyes, his knees up, his body relaxed. His Winchester sat propped against the wall. His breathing was measured. As he dozed he recalled his father's merry eyes and the wisp of gray hair at his temples. And in his sleep he saw himself, a gangly youth prone to long poker games and jugs of whiskey.

He opened his eyes and stirred. He had risen before the sun and made the trek back to town in the dark. It was necessary in order to avoid being caught in the open. His hiding place was a safe haven as long as he didn't move, therefore he determined his camp at Snakebite Creek would only be used as a refuge to sleep.

It was seven o'clock. The morning air was cool but already the heat was creeping back. Before long the heat would make another effort at suffocating the town. Tibbs licked his dry lips. He had chosen to rest here behind Mike's saloon because it would be the last place Hagard might look. He had not wanted to doze off and he cursed himself when he opened his eyes. He couldn't make any mistakes. Surviving his second day in Raven Flats would be an extraordinary challenge.

He was hungry. The water from his canteen and the dried beef jerky only went so far in quenching the howls from his belly. His stood and stretched. Following the alley along the backside of three buildings he came to a corner and glanced out at the street. A blackbird pecked at crumbs in the dust. Cutting between two buildings he came to the street and slipped on to the boardwalk. He was in front of Hart's Dry Goods & Clothing Store. Down the street he saw Grant, Pap's old yellow dog, lazing in the shade under the awning. There was no other sign of life. He was about to make for Pap's when a voice said, 'Cole!'

He spun and with lightning speed his rifle was leveled but the sight before him stopped him cold. The girl that stood in the doorway had chestnut hair and flashing green eyes, her voluptuous figure was outlined beneath her simple cotton dress by the morning light. She held a broom like a soldier holding a rifle at port arms.

'Cole Tibbs, I—'

'Shh!' Tibbs put his finger to his lips. 'Inside!'

She backed into the store and Tibbs shut the door behind them.

'Cole, I heard you were back in town. . . .' She glanced at the rifle in his hand. Tibbs tipped it away and eased the trigger down. 'You're a gunfighter now!'

It was her tone of voice that stung Tibbs.

You're a gunfighter now!

She said the words with undisguised rancor. Tibbs was momentarily stunned. Jamie Hart had been a gangly teenage girl when he left town seven years before, and they had been friends, although their relationship was strained because of his unruly lifestyle. Now she had grown into a breathtaking young woman who looked upon him with disgust.

'I can't believe this,' she continued. 'I heard you killed Sam Usher yesterday.'

'He pulled a gun. Listen Jamie, it's not like you think.'

'Not like I think! Why, I think you're a damn fool! You haven't amounted to anything. Get out of my store! The Ushers are going to kill you soon and I don't want your blood on my floor!'

Tibbs was about to pull his deputy marshal's star from his pocket and explain himself when a sound in the street caught their attention. A glance through the window revealed five men walking down the street. They kicked at the cawing ravens in the street and paused. Tibbs couldn't make out their words but they must have been discussing

44

their orders. Two men strolled past Pap's cantina and on toward a series of dilapidated adobe huts that comprised the east end. The other three ambled toward the train depot.

He turned again to Jamie Hart. 'I can't explain now, Jamie, but you'll have to trust me. . . .'

'Trust you!'

'I'm not a gunslinger but more blood will be spilled. It doesn't have to be that way but old man Usher started this years ago.'

'Get out of my store!'

'I'm going.' Tibbs took another glance at the street. The men were gone and it was time for him to move. 'I'm going out the back,' he said. 'I'd appreciate it if you didn't mention seeing me.'

'There's no law to speak of,' Jamie said. 'But if there was I'd have you arrested. And I hope I don't see you again!'

Tibbs studied her. Her eyes blazed with fury, but there was disappointment there, too. They had been friends once but Tibbs had turned to gambling and drinking. How could he tell her he wasn't the same man any longer? Silently, he went out the rear entrance without looking back, his jaw clenched tightly.

He wanted to get into Pap's cantina but the back alley was blocked by a fence. He had to move a barrel in place to climb over. A sprint across the boardwalk out front was too dangerous now that Usher's men were moving about. After dropping over the fence he skirted around an out-house and a utility shed. The rear entrance to Pap's cantina was thirty feet away but he would have to cross an open space to reach the door. The only danger lay in the two men that were watching from the adobe section just another fifty yards past Pap's.

He walked casually into the sunlight, just like another citizen running an errand. Onto the boardwalk and into the shade that fanned over Pap's cantina doorway, through the batwing doors, and only then did his fingers twitch inches from his gun. Pap was behind the bar. He looked up and said 'You're still alive.' He said it as a statement and Tibbs grinned.

'I hate to say I told you so.'

'But you told me so. And I reckon today should be mighty interesting.'

'And that it will be,' Tibbs promised. 'Can you make me up some breakfast?' Tibbs pulled a greenback from his trouser pocket and set it on the bar.

'I wouldn't deprive a doomed man his last meal.'

Pap scooted off his chair and went back to the kitchen. As he walked away Tibbs said, 'Thanks for the vote of confidence.'

Tibbs sat at a table facing the doorway. He didn't know how long it would be before Usher's men checked the cantina again, but they would certainly come. And just for a moment the anguish he had felt seven years earlier had returned; it hung before him like the shadows of the men that were now hunting him, a palpable and detrimental presence. So in his mind's eye he wrapped his fist about his anguish and smothered it. The shadows wavered in the blazing sunlight beyond the door, but just before they vanished a voice inside his head lamented *if only I had been a better man all those years ago. . . .* Tibbs tightened his grip and the anguish washed away with his blinking eyes.

Pap returned with a tin plate of scrambled eggs, burnt bacon, and a half a loaf of hard bread. He looked at Tibbs.

'You all right, pardner?'

'I'm fine,' Tibbs growled.

He ate without looking up, quickly, and with the hunger of a wolf. When he was finished Pap served him coffee and Tibbs sat back and watched the door.

'Anybody ever tell you what a damn fool you are?' Pap asked.

'They have.'

'Good. I didn't want there to be any misconceptions here.'

'There aren't.'

They both watched the sunlight past the batwing doors. The street was bathed in a golden light and Tibbs could feel the heat begin to accumulate.

'Your father was a hell of a fightin' man,' Pap said at last. 'I never saw anyone that loved the army so.'

'I can't change what happened,' Tibbs said. 'But I can bring Usher to justice.'

Pap was thoughtful. Then he said, 'I expect you'll be dead by noon. But I will say the stories I heard about you have given me pause.'

Tibbs looked the old man over and in his craggy face he saw the fierce young soldier that had fought side by side with his father at Bull Run. Here was his past etched in those wrinkled features, proud and unrelenting, and once again he felt the anguish of his misspent youth and again he willed the anguish into submission. Tibbs pulled the deputy US marshal's star from his pocket and pinned it on to his vest. Pap's eyes went wide.

'That boy you knew is dead,' Tibbs said. 'I killed him like they killed my father. Nothing I can say or do can make the past right, so if you don't mind I'll concentrate on making today right. It's all I have.'

Pap let out a low whistle from between his lips. 'I'll be damned! You're working as a US marshal!'

'A deputy US marshal.'

'Deputy or not, the last seven years surely must have been something!'

'That they were.'

'And I heard you were fighting alongside Ethan O'Hara up in Wyoming.'

'That's true.'

'And Maxfield Knight, the man they say hunted down the last of Quantrill's raiders.'

At the mention of Knight's name Tibbs raised an eyebrow. 'True, and Knight's on his way here.'

'Jumpin' Jesus!'

Pap grabbed a brown bottle from the bar, uncorked it, and took a long swallow. He coughed and hacked, glanced at Tibbs, and took another long draw from the bottle.

'Bless my bones! This is better than a night dancing with a Tijuana dove after winning two hands of poker!'

Tibbs thought Pap was about to leap in the air and kick his heels.

'By God those mule-eared bastard sons of Usher are gonna pay! Why, this changes everything!'

'Ease up, Pap. This has to be done right.'

'Done right? Why you crazy loon! You'll be lucky to survive the morning! The way I see it we have to plan this out together and keep you alive!'

'No.'

The tone in his voice stopped Pap cold.

'No?'

'I can't put anyone at risk. You stay out of it.'

48

Pap sat back and examined Tibbs. 'You tell me this news and won't accept my help. That star on your vest won't keep you alive. You need help. Don't you understand that?'

'Did my father ever ask for help?'

Pap nodded slowly. 'I get it. Well, you're still a damned fool.'

'I suppose so.'

Pap pulled his corncob pipe from his pocket and thumbed tobacco into it from a small leather pouch. He struck a match and inhaled. The tobacco flared and blue smoke rose like question marks into the air.

'Your pa and I knew a sergeant named O'Reilly who smoked a hand-carved Meerschaum pipe. He died at Bull Run. He was a big Irish bastard and fearless. He took a musket ball in the heart but kept charging. Never saw anything like it before or since.'

'I recall my father mentioning O'Reilly.'

'There was something about the army that your father loved.' Pap's features had softened and the crow's feet near his eyes wrinkled into a faint smile as the memories came to life. 'I think he enjoyed the discipline. It was all boots and saddles but there was honor and love of country. This land is a gift; the Apache know it and the Arapaho and Cheyenne know it. General Washington knew it during the War of Independence, but too many have forgotten.'

Pap chewed on his pipe stem, the heady aroma of tobacco filling the room. The tobacco smoke reminded Tibbs of his father and he had to suppress his own memories again. But as Pap reminisced he recalled his father in his den, the very room now occupied by old man Usher.

Tibbs set down his coffee cup because his hand had begun to shake with rage.

'Your pa loved this country. He loved what it stood for. The dream that we can all live here in peace will never die, but sometimes we have to fight to keep it alive. I think your pa would be right proud to see you wearing that star on your vest.'

Tibbs picked up his cup and his hand was steady again. He finished the coffee and set the cup down sharply on the table. He stood up, picked up the Winchester and started for the door. Surprised, Pap leapt to his feet.

'Where the hell are you going?'

Tibbs paused and looked at Pap. 'It's time I let folks know I'm a lawman. There's no sense keeping it a secret and it might save a few lives. Some of those boys might think twice before drawing on a deputy US marshal.'

Pap chuckled. 'Don't bet on it.'

Tibbs pushed through the batwing doors and into the blazing street. He glanced at Jamie Hart's storefront. There was no sign of the beautiful but angry young woman that had sent him packing less than an hour earlier.

He made his way past the Fool's Gold Saloon and on to a hitching post in front of the Pioneer restaurant. Several horses were tied to the post and they raised their heads from the water trough as he approached. The horses all carried the Usher brand. The sound of voices emanating from the restaurant was so loud that Tibbs wondered why they hadn't posted a guard. They were being careless, he thought, and overconfident.

He crossed on to the boardwalk and peeked over the batwing doors. Eight men sat at three tables having breakfast, They were all Usher's men. Two waitresses were handling the raucous crowd. There was a noticeable lack of townspeople in a restaurant usually crowded with townies at this time of the morning. Bret Hagard sat at the furthest table. Tibbs would have to handle the men closest to the door first.

Hagard was ruddy-faced, tall, and wiry. His unshaven face added to the appearance of unseemliness that clung to the man like trail dust. His eyes were blue but humorless, lacking vitality. They were cold, hard eyes like glass marbles. Tibbs had never liked the man. There was simply something evil about Hagard. He jacked a round into his Winchester and flung himself through the batwing doors.

Bounding into the room he slammed into the first table and with a sweep of his rifle he knocked a man from his chair, brought the rifle around and blew a hole through the first man that had drawn his gun. The waitresses screamed and ran for cover. Amid the turmoil that ensued another man pulled a gun and Tibbs shot the man in the shoulder. Bone and blood burst from the man's shirt and he dropped his gun, tumbling to the floor screaming.

Leaping past the table he kicked the next table over, raked his rifle across a man's mouth, knocking out a bloody clatter of teeth. He propelled himself past the table and pulled over Hagard's table with his left hand, keeping the rifle steady in his right hand, shouting at Hagard, 'Pull your gun, Hagard! Pull that hogleg!'

So quickly had all of this occurred that Hagard was caught by surprise, a forkful of scrambled eggs poised at his mouth. By the time Tibbs had reached his table his hand had dropped to his holster and he was looking down the barrel of a Winchester.

The sound of the two rifle shots still echoed off the

51

plank walls, the moans of the injured mingling with the harsh, rasping voice of Cole Tibbs.

'Nothing would give me more pleasure than to blow you into eternity, Hagard. Just give me a reason.'

Boots scuffled against the greasy floorboards, chairs creaked and one of the waitresses sobbed. Tibbs was acutely aware of the men converging behind him but his gaze never wavered from Hagard.

'If I hear one hammer being pulled back I'll shoot.'

Sweat dribbled from under Hagard's Stetson. He slowly raised his hand away from his holster.

'Back off boys. Let's hear the man out.'

The room was silent but for the grunts of the two injured men. Hagard's eyes dropped to the star on Tibbs' vest.

'What's this? You're a lawman now?'

'Pay attention to what I'm about to say,' Tibbs rasped. 'I'm a deputy US marshal and I'm here on official business. Stay out of my way or I'll kill you.'

'You can't be serious? Usher wants you dead! You won't last out the afternoon!'

'You've been warned.'

Hagard's expression changed from an incredulous stare to astonished mirth. He burst out laughing.

'Haw! Now I've seen everything! The drunk kid makes good and returns home wearing a badge, why you're no better than your stinkin' pa—'

With a mighty sweep of his arms Tibbs swung the Winchester stock into Hagard's jaw cutting a red swath across his mouth. He was rocked back and nearly toppled backward off the chair. His eyes squeezed shut in pain and his hand instinctively groped for his gun. Tibbs brought the rifle around again and slammed the stock on to Hagard's nose shattering it. He howled in pain and Tibbs kicked him off his chair. As Hagard lay writhing on the ground he yanked his gun from his holster and quickly turned to face the crowd.

'You boys all heard what I had to say. Stay out of my way and leave me to my business. I won't hesitate to shoot any one of you bastards if you give me reason.'

And with that Tibbs strolled from the restaurant stepping over the body of the sixth man he'd killed since returning to Raven Flats.

CHAPTER FIVE

The great locomotive rumbled across the southwest, belching black smoke that trailed behind it like thunderclouds, its wheels clattering across the gleaming tracks and its engine chugging loudly until the air was filled with a steady hum and the sound of its lonesome whistle announcing its arrival like some iron beast come to conquer the land. The Sioux, Cheyenne and Arapaho had long lamented the intrusion of this Iron Horse that howled like a giant metal monster across their sacred land; as time passed they accepted their way of life was ending, as all things must end and become transformed into something else. For the Indians the Iron Horse was a symbol of the white man's endurance and the coming of their years in exile, strangers in their own land. For US Marshal Maxfield Knight the locomotive was a reminder of the long journeys during the war; of sleepless nights on troop trains and midnight raids against Confederate railyard munitions warehouses.

He sat in the dining car watching the blistering desert sweep past the window, the slight rocking of the train a monotonous sway that put him on edge. He drank coffee and listened to the idle chatter of the other passengers. His US marshal's badge was in his pocket as Tibbs and him had agreed. It was important the presence of lawmen in the territory remain secret until the last possible moment. If the Ushers learned of their presence they would surely piece together the facts and flee. Knight and Tibbs wanted swift justice, not a prolonged battle.

He wondered how Tibbs had fared. The kid was stubborn but far above average in intelligence. He was quick with a gun and good with his fists. Knight had no doubt that Tibbs had survived his first day in Raven Flats, but this was the second day and from what Knight knew about the Ushers it would be a long, hot day for Cole Tibbs.

Knight had warned Tibbs about leaving before him, and he regretted that his obligations in Montana had prevented him from joining Tibbs. Still, the kid was strong-willed and capable of handling himself. He'd proven that a dozen times. In fact, Knight's delay had proven fortuitous. As he sipped his coffee and mused on the beauty of the ocotillo and cactus that swept past the window, two men slipped into the dining car and took a table twenty feet from him.

Les and Edgar Usher.

Knight picked up the newspaper from his white linen table and motioned the waiter for more coffee. With another steaming cup before him he feigned interest in the news. Now here was something that he never thought he'd live to see. The modern world had caught up with the lonely stretches of land west of the Mississippi and now he sat in a dining car hurtling across the vast reaches of this grand country, sipping coffee and reading the newspaper like some dignified dandy back in one of New York's finest restaurants. And all while preparing to arrest two highly skilled and dangerous embezzlers who sat not twenty feet away eating their chicken dinner and drinking wine with the same pretense of aristocracy that made train travel so alluring. Knight thought the scene was surreal. In fact, he was downright flabbergasted.

He used the opportunity to study the brothers. Les was fair haired and balding. His skin was pock-marked and his dark eyebrows were in contrast to his light hair. The eyebrows reminded Knight of a stage actor's make-up and the effect gave Les Usher the appearance of a fancy boy. Edgar was similarly balding, but with darker hair and a crooked nose. Both men were just plain ugly, Knight thought.

Physically neither man was a threat to Knight or Tibbs. These two were thin, gaunt looking men with little muscle; their spare frames would collapse under the barrage from Knight's fists. But no matter their unimpressive frames, Knight accepted that Les and Edgar Usher were equally as dangerous as any adversary he'd faced. In each set of emotionless eyes there flickered an unholy light that Knight had seen in few men. It was a cast to their demeanor, that dark flame in their pupils, and wicked curl of their lips that convinced him that these two men were capable – if not guilty – of cold blooded murder.

Their presence on the train with Knight was a lucky accident. A few greenbacks slipped into the black porter's palm confirmed that these two were indeed the Usher brothers. No doubt their father had summoned them once Cole Tibbs made himself known. Knight wondered if Tibbs had kept his identity as a lawman secret. It seemed unlikely the kid could manage this long without revealing his legal right. It would be necessary to save lives.

Satisfied that he'd seen enough of the Ushers for one day, Knight retired to his private room. The small bunk was sufficient for sleeping but the damn clatter of the tracks was irritating. He could never get used to it.

He pulled up the shade so he could watch the landscape breeze past, a blur of brown, green, blue, and orange that wavered outside the glass like a mirage. The sun was high and the desert was bristling with heat. The room was warm and Knight removed his coat. He unbuckled his gunbelt and draped it across the opposite bunk. He'd paid extra to have the double sleeping room to himself.

He pulled his gun from the holster and gauged its weight in his hand. The Colt was custom made with a seven-inch barrel. The walnut stock was a rich dark brown, the blue metal gleaming with a thin sheen of oil. Knight had cleaned the gun only yesterday. The Colt Single-Action Army revolver was the finest handgun in existence. Neither the Remington revolver nor the Smith & Wesson had the same feel for Knight. The Colt had served him well against bank robbers, stage robbers, murderers, and crazed half-breeds for ten years now. He knew with certainty it was about to be used again.

He holstered the gun and lay back on the bunk. Damn, I must be getting old, he thought, because now I've taken to napping in the afternoon. But Knight's afternoon sleep was restless, his mind conjuring images of the past and mingling them with those of the present. When his eyelids fluttered closed he had wished to see an image of his long dead wife but instead he drifted into Georgia again when he marched with Sherman toward Atlanta. And then Atlanta burned and the sky was blood red and the heavy scent of smoke and charred bodies drifted across the years and he heard the bugle's reveille before opening his eyes again.

The southwestern landscape rolled past the window. In that half-dream state, lumbering toward wakefulness, he thought of Tibbs and how the young man had told him about his father's murder.

He drifted off again, his eyes blinking away the southwestern sunlight, his memory conjuring an image of Tibbs. Knight had liked the kid right away. He was a kindred spirit, perhaps, and Knight understood all too well the anguish that comes from violence. Tibbs had endured much, had been ridiculed for his slovenly ways, and had witnessed his father's murder. And like Knight, he hadn't given up.

He opened his eyes. Pulling the gold watch from his pocket he checked the time. He'd barely slept thirty minutes. The constant motion of the train, the anticipation of the coming battle, and certainly the ever present memories of past battles, all nagged at Knight's troubled mind.

He wanted to complete this assignment and see to it that Tibbs put the past behind him. And putting the past behind him was something that Knight himself had never managed.

Yet for Tibbs this wasn't simply another assignment, it was a personal matter, and Knight had allowed his participation knowing he couldn't stop him; Tibbs would have gone after the Ushers on his own. Another day and Knight would arrive in Raven Flats. At least this way he could provide legal support. The plan might even work.

But Knight knew their success was dependent on how much trouble Cole Tibbs had found for himself.

CHAPTER SIX

Trouble was coming for Tibbs early that very afternoon. Once outside the Pioneer restaurant he tossed Hagard's gun into the horse trough and began making his way toward the train depot. His goal was to confront the sentries posted there and advise them to stand down. And Tibbs, being a rational man, understood fully the unlikelihood of that occurrence. Still, he had to try.

He had taken but a few steps when a man emerged from an alley and crossed into the street. He stopped, waiting for Tibbs. In that same instant another man emerged from behind a building and also entered the dusty street, but behind Tibbs. This man also halted in the street. Neither man carried a rifle but the low-slung guns on the hips and their demeanor spoke volumes about their readiness.

Tibbs wasn't particularly concerned. He didn't feel boxed in at all even though this was their intention. With nary a pause he shrugged and began walking calmly toward the man in front of him. He carried his Winchester in his right hand. He knew the man would soon see the star on his vest as he closed the gap.

The man that waited twitched his fingers. Tibbs smiled. This had an odd effect on the man and Tibbs thought he'd rattled him by smiling. They were expecting a one-sided gunfight and not a smiling lawman. The man had a face that reminded him of sawdust: his skin was mottled and bristling with several days of growth; his eyes were the gray of tin and equally as flat and devoid of intelligence.

Tibbs smiled again and said, 'Mornin,' pardner. I'm Deputy US Marshal Tibbs. I just arrived yesterday and I'd like to ask that you stay out of my way while I'm in town.'

Those gray eyes widened as the man fathomed the meaning of the words.

'It isn't all that hard to figure,' Tibbs continued. 'I'm going to arrest the Usher brothers once they get back to town and I don't want any unnecessary bloodshed. The bodies do seem to be piling up mighty fast and I'd hate to add your carcass to the pile.'

When Tibbs spoke he kept his voice even, pronouncing his words carefully and he was conscious of avoiding any movement that might be deemed threatening. But he had already guessed the man's reaction, for Carleton Usher paid his men well for their loyalty.

'Why you—!' the man exclaimed, reaching for his gun.

Tibbs slammed the Winchester's stock into the man's belly, knocking the air from his lungs and doubling him over. The man spat, 'Oof!' and Tibbs swept the rifle across his head, knocking him unconscious. Without hesitation he spun, levered a round into the breech and shot the man behind him in the leg. The man yowled in pain, his Colt firing uselessly at the ground as he fell.

Then Tibbs was running.

Bounding on to the boardwalk he raced along the slats, kicking up dust as he went, and then, remarkably, he stopped.

The men watching from the street stared gape-jawed as Tibbs brought himself up to the abandoned sheriff's office and flung open the door. To the further astonishment of the men he strolled into the office without a backward glance.

Inside the office, Tibbs perused the room. Dust covered the furniture. There was an old desk that Tibbs knew once belonged to Sheriff Barton Connors, a kind old lawman who died the same night as his father. The chair had been overturned and he righted it, sweeping aside a half dozen yellowing Wanted posters. The cells' keys still hung on a peg but the gun rack was empty. He placed his Winchester on the gun rack and surveyed the back room. He found a slop bucket and broom. He brought the broom out to the front. He nodded to himself. There was a lot of work to do.

As he worked sweeping out the office he gave no thought to the men he'd just killed or the wounded whose screams still lingered on the hot, dry wind. After twenty minutes he had the office in a presentable condition. There was no mattress for the springboard frame in the jail's solitary cell, but he could rectify that later.

He found an extra chair in the back room and he set that outside the door on the boardwalk. He sat in the chair and smoked a cigarette. After ten minutes he heard the hoofbeats. He looked up and saw that Hagard and his men had mounted their horses. The man he'd killed in the restaurant was draped over a mule. The injured sat forlornly astride their mounts. Hagard's nose was swollen and his eyes were puffed with tears. They all glared at Tibbs.

For a moment Tibbs felt isolated although he was unafraid. An image of his father flashed through his mind and he watched Hagard and the other riders put the spurs to their horses and ride from town. The sun was high in the afternoon sky and the heat was once again piling up around him. His cigarette smoke lingered in the air, finally drifting heavenward in a ghostly dance of sun-dappled motion.

He tossed the cigarette butt into the dust where it was immediately besieged by two blackbirds that sank into the street like harbingers of death. Tibbs had to resist the urge to shoot the birds.

With his Winchester on the rack in the office and the Colt in his holster he was confident of handling any sudden attacks, but that was unlikely now. They had retreated and Hagard would face old man Usher. He would explain as best he could why Tibbs was still alive. The conversation would not be easy for any of them.

But Tibbs also knew this was only the beginning.

Jamie Hart emerged from her storefront and peered in his direction. He waved. She turned on her heel and disappeared into her store. So much for that.

He waited, hoping that she would emerge again. The blackbirds had given up on his cigarette butt and fluttered away.

On the opposite side of the street Pap Wingfoot emerged from his cantina and strolled toward Tibbs. He was carrying his shotgun. He went into the office and brought out the other chair. They sat together watching the street. Other than the blackbirds there was no sign of life. The town appeared deserted although they both knew each building was bustling within.

'Heard some shooting,' Pap finally said.

'I killed one in the restaurant and busted Hagard's nose. They all hightailed it for the ranch.'

'Old man Usher is gonna be stewed.'

'That he is.'

Pap's old dog, Grant, ambled down the street, came up to Tibbs, and sniffed his boots. He wagged his tail and plopped on to the boardwalk at Pap's feet for a nap.

'Six or seven dead so far,' Pap said.

'I wasn't counting.'

'The Mexicans should leave you alone.'

'They will. I spoke with Feliciano. *Nada y pues nada.*'

Tibbs tilted his chair back and he stretched out with his boots resting on the hitching rail.

'The way I see it, Hagard and the boys will start hitting the whiskey. Then they're all bound to saddle up and come out here. Usher can get fifty men together.'

'Let's be optimistic,' Tibbs said.

'Optimistic?'

'He might get twenty men together at the most. Hagard will lead the charge, but not all of them will come because they're not all bloodthirsty curs. So I figure at least twenty.'

Pap frowned. 'That's optimistic?'

'It is.'

'Well, you're just like your pa.'

Tibbs glanced at Pap and then back at the street. Grant snoozed at their feet. A warm breeze teased them and then slipped away. The heat continued to pile up.

'I had a wife once,' Pap said. 'I met her in San Antonio.

64

I rode for some time with a gunman named Wade Hatton. She was his sister. She had a figure like an hourglass and looked pretty. She died of fever before we could get married. I would have enjoyed finding another woman but now I'm too old.'

Tibbs wasn't certain what to say so he remained silent.

'Along with your pa I've known men that were fast with a gun. Hickok, Hatton, Dillon and Earp. They were all fast. This fella Max Knight is suppose to be one tough hombre. How well do you know him?'

'Well enough.'

'When does he get here to save your sorry ass?'

'He said he'd be on tomorrow's train.'

'Les and Edgar could be on that train.'

'That's the way I figured it.'

'Of course you've got yourself a plan. It must be one of those secret lawman plans that you boys come up with.'

'Right.' Tibbs had to chuckle.

'You haven't been real forthcoming about the details.'

'No, I haven't.'

Pap ran his hand along his shotgun. 'This old greener has stopped stage robbers and Chiricahua.'

'Stay out of it.'

'No sir, I won't.'

Tibbs looked at the sky. The blue horizon stretched from the glimmering desert to the distant mountains; the sun was hot and white and the glare beat down on Raven Flats with such ferocity he expected the storefronts and boardwalk to burst into flames. He removed his Stetson, untied the bandanna around his neck, and mopped the perspiration from his face.

Once again Jamie Hart emerged from her storefront.

She looked up and down the street, carefully avoiding making eye contact with Tibbs who was prepared to wave again if she did. Instead, she began to slowly sweep the dust from the boardwalk. She wore a simple blue cotton dress and her chestnut hair caught the light and glimmered for a moment like strands of gold. Tibbs felt a lump in his throat. He could see the outline of her figure through the thin fabric. Pap looked at Jamie.

'You talk to her yet?' he asked.

'Briefly.'

'She only remembers the drunk kid that got chased out of town. Might be a good time to talk with her.'

'Not today.'

'If you get killed I'm certain she'll place flowers on your grave.'

'I feel better already,' Tibbs said sarcastically. Pap chuckled.

Tibbs recalled the day Jamie had taken him riding in a buckboard with a wicker basket of fried chicken and boiled potatoes. They had set out a blanket not far from Snakebite Creek, and after lunch he had kissed her once, quickly and hotly, her lips tasting like potatoes, and she had blushed furiously but never objected. That afternoon the desert was alive with color and sound and a blackbird fled across the sky showing a spot of red under its quick wing. Jamie laughed and a breeze caught the edge of her hair and it touched his cheek. Her eyes danced with an inner light and she told him all about the books she'd read; Dickens and Longfellow and Shakespeare, and how she wanted to have children some day so that she might read to them. A career as a teacher was but a dream, and she dreamed avidly of leaving Raven Flats to better her life. They walked along the creek admiring the desert flowers and wild cactus that bloomed so beautifully from such a harsh

66

and uncompromising landscape, but that day there was nothing uncompromising or harsh about a day spent in the sun. She held his hand as they walked and he felt a thrill run through him. Three weeks later he was drunk two days straight and losing at poker when his father was killed by Sam Usher not far from the place where they had made their picnic, the sound of rattlesnakes filling the sunlight with their grating sound. The Usher boys had forced his father to sign over the deed to their land, had killed him, and found Cole in the saloon, far too drunk to defend himself. They had beaten him, laughing as they did so, tied him to a mule and paraded him along the street and out of town. Remembering this he let out his breath and fought against the grief that gripped his heart as he blinked away the sunlight and concentrated on the blackbirds that dropped soundlessly into the street like mocking spirits. . . .

The door to Jamie's store slammed shut with the force of a pistol shot.

'She's mighty agitated now that you're back,' Pap said.

'We'll work it out later.'

Tibbs concentrated on the task that he faced and examined his options from every angle. Pap smoked his corncob pipe and presented an impression of a man without a care in the world. But Tibbs knew he was thinking about it, too. So the two of them sat together silently in the shade as the sun blazed down and Grant's tail swished away an occasional fly. Finally, Tibbs pulled a roll of greenbacks from his vest pocket and peeled off several bills. He handed them to Pap.

'What's this for?'

'I need lamp oil for the sheriff's office, and an extra lamp to go with it.'

'Why don't you go buy it your own self? Miss Hart would

be downright tickled if you ambled over there right now and straightened things out with her.'

'No, you do it. I have to reconnoiter.'

'What the hell are you going to reconnoiter?'

'Things.'

'Things! The town's empty of bad-asses for at least a few hours. And the people that live here are staying inside until after the shooting stops. And I don't have to remind you the shooting is gonna start again at sundown! Reconnoitering don't make sense to me. You need to come up with a plan to keep you alive!'

'I have one,' Tibbs said, rising to his feet. 'It's a secret lawman's plan. Just get that lamp and the oil.'

He left Pap chuckling on the boardwalk and made for the adobe section of town. After twenty minutes he was satisfied that none of Usher's men were left behind and repeated his search of the train depot and cattle pens. A few curious faces spied upon him from windows and from the shaded doorways, but none of the townspeople approached him. Tibbs figured it was nearly one hundred degrees in the shade. His shirt was damp with perspiration and his Stetson felt heavy and hot on his head, but removing it was out of the question because of what the sun could do to a man's scalp in five minutes.

The skyline shimmered in the heat and the mountains in the north looked like a scene painted for a magazine cover. The distant purple was ridged with the white smear of snow, an innocuous sight that reminded him that nature was fascinating, bewildering, and uncaring.

He returned to the sheriff's office and waited for Pap to return with the lamp and oil, all the while wondering what Pap had said to Jamie, and what she might possibly think about all of this. He forced the thought aside because he knew the setting sun would bring night riders, and with them rode death.

CHAPTER SEVEN

They came after sunset, a wave of galloping hoof beats that thundered across the desert, the whoops and battle cries of Hagard and his men echoing across the vast desert. Tibbs had struck a lucifer to his trousers and had lit both lamps. Positioning them on the desk, and with the curtains pulled, a yellow glow would seep from the window and distract Hagard and the boys just long enough. By the time the galloping hoofbeats drew near, Tibbs was walking toward the adobe section of town.

Pap followed without speaking. They crossed the adobe section and came to a ravine that bordered the north end of Raven Flats.

'Is this where we make our last stand?' Pap asked. 'Doggone it boy! This is a worse place to fight than Custer hill!'

'We're not going to fight them,' Tibbs said.

'What the hell does that mean?'

'It means we stay alive tonight. No fighting.'

'And how in the name of Ulysses S. Grant do you intend on staying alive without fighting?' Pap couldn't believe what he was hearing.

'We run.' Tibbs said, gesturing toward the darkening desert that lay before them.

And so they did.

The entered the desert at twilight. This was an obstinate land, where the fragility of life is told by a bleached coyote's skull. During the day this is a blasted panorama teeming with life but invoking death. At night the heat waves dissipate into towering shadows where a man could get lost in mere minutes. But Tibbs knew his way through this deceptive landscape. He led Pap into a grove of creosote bush where they blended into the darkness, and waited.

They heard the sound of angry voices followed by gunshots as Hagard and his men took the bait and fired upon an empty sheriff's office. The volley of gunfire echoed across the rows of cholla cactus at precisely the same moment a coyote began its melodic yipping in the distance.

The desert sand whispered with the sound of their boots pressing across a swale as Tibbs led them deeper into the darkness.

'Where are we going?' Pap whispered.

'Snakebite Creek.'

'You're a damn fool.'

Damn fool or not, Pap followed, eager for battle and curious as to why Tibbs was leading them in a large circle that sent them not only toward Snakebite Creek, but closer to the Usher ranch.

A barrel cactus loomed before them. The cactus was huge, at least twelve feet tall, its limbs stretching out like a spirit's arms probing the darkness. The stars had begun to populate the sky and a sliver of moon offered little light.

71

The distant mountains, which during the daylight appeared to float like shimmering islands, were now nothing more than the shadows of hulking giants.

Tibbs paused, listening. The gunfire had ceased and then for a while all they heard were angry shouts. Now silence enveloped them. Tibbs knew Hagard and his men would search every building, but it would take time.

'Hagard might send a rider to circle the town as a chance of finding us.'

'Not in this darkness,' Pap said.

'No, they won't find us as long as we remain silent. We can't shoot either. The muzzle flash would reveal our position. And from here on we move slowly.'

Tibbs couldn't see that Pap was grinning from ear to ear, nor did he have any way of knowing the old timer was thinking that his father would be right proud of his son. Then they moved past the cactus and began circling toward Snakebite Creek. A shooting star blazed briefly across the star-clotted heavens and Tibbs made a wish just as he had so many times in his youth. He felt confident and determined as they traversed the first two hundred yards in a wide circle away from Raven Flats.

Pap heard it first.

The snicker of a horse followed by the clip-clop of a hoof on sand.

They froze.

Tibbs held his Winchester firmly in his right hand and resisted the urge to lever a round into the breech.

Silence. As they stood listening to the darkness the air itself seemed to blacken; night falls quickly in the desert. The warm breeze carried the scent of sand, cactus, and the dry, lingering scent of gunpowder that must surely have risen to the breeze from Raven Flats.

Fifty yards on his left a lucifer flared to life as the rider swept it across his knee. The cigarette sent the aroma of tobacco off on to the breeze.

'The fool,' Pap whispered. 'We could blow him out of his saddle at any time.'

'Probably had a few snorts of whiskey,' Tibbs said. 'Let's sit tight and wait him out.'

The rider smoked his cigarette and eventually spurred his horse into a wide circle. His silhouette stood out against the starry horizon. As the night deepened the chance of seeing anyone in the tangle of cactus and brush was eliminated and the rider gave up his sentry duty and returned to town. Tibbs waited until he was satisfied they were alone again and then nudged Pap.

Crossing the whispering sands they came at last to the rock strewn perimeter of Snakebite Creek. Two hours had passed since Hagard and his men had assaulted the abandoned sheriff's office. Raven Flats glimmered in the distance, silent and foreboding. On the opposite side a few yellow lights shone through the distant windows of Usher's hacienda. They climbed over the rocks and Tibbs led Pap into the crevice where he'd left his saddle-bag.

'Have a seat,' Tibbs offered. 'It's not much but it's home.'

Pap chuckled. 'So this is where you've been hiding. Right in the middle of everything!'

'Tomorrow we sleep in town,' Tibbs said.

'How do you figure?'

Tibbs told him the plan he'd outlined with Max Knight. Pap listened intently and when Tibbs was finished he whistled between his teeth. 'Hooray! You're either gonna get us all killed or make territorial history!'

'One way or the other,' Tibbs said, 'tomorrow will settle a lot.'

'Why didn't you just arrest old man Usher right off?'

'We don't have warrants on him. It's Edgar and Les that we want. If he'd known I was with the marshal's service he would have warned them to stay away. Now they're on their way here.'

'And you must have been hoping the old man would have pulled a gun on you.'

Tibbs frowned. 'He's broken either way.'

'But Hagard is someone you'll have to deal with, too.'

Pap settled down against the rocks, his shotgun propped next to him. Shortly he was snoring and Tibbs rose up and looked out across the swelling blackness as the creek trickled along eternally with a sound like whispering mourners. The desert had taken on the hue of an apocalypse, empty and alone. He waited patiently for morning, brushing aside thoughts of Jamie Hart's slender figure and flashing eyes, his pulse hammering like a metronome, and he felt the soft desert wind touch his brow and nudge him along a violent path that he knew stretched away from the bunched up darkness toward the cold breaking of dawn.

CHAPTER EIGHT

Nineteen years earlier Maxfield Knight had been with Sherman's troops when they began their summer assault against Atlanta, and unknown to him at the time Carleton Usher was fighting valiantly with the rebels, galloping astride a gray horse while flashing his saber and screaming, 'Hold your ranks, boys! We'll rally now! Drive those heathen blue bellies back to Chicago!' In the ensuing years Usher had been plotting a lifetime of murder. The musket fire echoed across the years as Knight slept fitfully in his private room, the clatter of the train working at his nerves with the tenacity of restless ghosts.

He was aware, of course, of Usher's Confederate military record, and he set out on this assignment with the knowledge that he was once again facing an old enemy no matter that the two men had never met. He was resigned to the fact that he would never stop fighting that war, and that one day in all likelihood he would fail and die a violent death like that which he had delivered to so many outlaws over the years. But not this time.

General Sherman's flinty profile emerged in his dream like a corpse floating upwards from the bottom of a deep pond, and his voice thundered across time: '*Let us destroy Atlanta and make it a desolation.*' And then he was in the thick of it again, the Confederates charging, their razor-sharp bayonets glinting in the late afternoon sun.

A knock at the door broke his reverie. He pulled himself up from the dregs of sleep, grumpy and sweating. He opened the door and greeted the porter with 'What is it?'

'The two men, sir. As you requested, I have kept an eye on them. I believe they have armed themselves. We'll be in Raven Flats in four hours.'

'What time is it?'

'Three twenty-five a.m., sir.'

Knight slipped the porter a greenback, and the porter, briefly appraising the man's hard features, nodded his thanks and slipped away. Knight shut the door and sat on the bunk. Darkness flashed past the window in endless waves. He saw himself in the window's reflection. His dark hair and walrus mustache were flecked with silver, his eyes had bags under them. Damn trains. Maybe he would get a good night's rest in Raven Flats.

He pulled his Colt from the holster on his right hip, flipped open the loading gate and punched out five cartridges. He checked the muzzle for any obstruction even though he knew the gun was clean – he had cleaned it himself less than twenty-four hours before. He replaced the cartridges and eased the hammer down on an empty cylinder. From his vest pocket he retrieved a two-shot derringer, and after checking this is as well he settled back and tried to clear his mind.

Tibbs had a '73 Winchester and if they needed extra rifles they could take them off of any dead men that lay in their path. The months of piecing together the trail of embezzlement that was culminating in this showdown were drawing to a close, and while Knight felt secure that the warrants folded into his coat pocket would result in a conviction of the Usher brothers, he doubted they would surrender peacefully. The witnesses to testify against them were in place, the depositions filed, and the warrants signed by a judge. But all of that meant nothing out here in the blistering southwest where disagreements were settled with a gun.

He went to the dining car and ordered coffee. He was alone but for another porter. He gave the porter a large tip and thanked him for keeping the coffee warm. The dining car officially closed at eight o'clock the previous evening but Knight wanted to take one last look around. The Ushers brothers would be in their room, probably sleeping. He wasn't surprised that they may have armed themselves. They were returning to Raven Flats expecting to kill Tibbs if their father's men hadn't done the job first.

The porter sat on one end of the long coach and Knight the other. Knight estimated the porter was about his age, and the southern tint to the man's voice had not escaped his notice. He drank his coffee and waited, expecting nothing and everything. He went over the train layout in his mind's eye, and he calculated the disembarkation at Raven Flats and how he would handle it.

He finished his coffee and gestured for the porter to bring another cup. Shortly, he set a steaming cup on the table watching Knight curiously.

'What is it?' Knight asked.

'I saw you once in El Paso. Maybe three years after the war. You pulled on two men and killed them before they could pull the hammer back.'

'Friends of yours?'

'No sir. I was passing through. But I've heard a lot of stories about you. The Yankee lawman that never gives up.'

'Get to the point.'

Knight was aware of the man's hands. They hung loosely at his sides and there was nothing in his demeanor that gave Knight reason to worry; the man was unarmed. But his voice had grown cold.

'I was captured by General Grant's men at Champion Hill near Vicksburg. I was in a Yankee prison when I learned my brother had died in Atlanta. I read in those magazines you rode with Sherman to Atlanta.'

'And all the way to the sea.'

'My brother was the last of my kinfolk.'

'The war's been over a long time.'

'Not for you, sir.'

Knight was suddenly tired. The man's anguish wouldn't be appeased after all of these years, and there was nothing Knight could do for either of them.

'A lot of good men died on both sides. I'm glad the war is over.'

'No sir, it isn't. You came on to this train carrying a gun and following two men we both know you'll kill. The engineer is a man named Delacroix who fought at Manassas. He's got a shotgun and I have an old Navy revolver back in my bunk. You start any trouble on this train and we'll shoot you down. In the meantime, if you need any more coffee you can continue giving me those greenbacks. I'll enjoy spending your money on a Yankee whore.'

The porter turned on his heel and strode across the

coach to resume his solitary vigil as Knight drank his coffee. The train seemed incredibly silent and Knight's temples throbbed as he controlled his anger. There was no sense getting into an argument with the man. The porter picked up a newspaper and feigned interest in the front page. Knight set several greenbacks on the table, stood up, and said across the coach, 'Enjoy yourself.'

He strode back to his room and sat on the bunk to watch the darkness clatter past the window, the sway and jostle of the train more irritating than ever.

He tried not to think about anything then for a long time. He dozed sitting upright on his bunk, his face reflected in the window, and eventually the pane of blackness behind the glass began to lighten and he heard the train's whistle blow. The landscape emerged from the bowl of night and the desert whipped past his window as if propelled by a demon wind.

He rubbed the sleep out of his eyes and yawned. He heard the porter call out 'Raven Flats!', the train decreased its speed, and the desert pulled up outside the window like a brown baked pictograph. He didn't care any longer about the porter's grief or even his own haunted memories, for Knight possessed the unique ability to concentrate on his objective when under duress. Now he understood that he would act only when he saw Tibbs.

And he knew one thing with certainty. Les and Edgar Usher were either on their way to Yuma or an early grave. Somehow Knight had a feeling the undertaker in Raven Flats would be kept busy.

CHAPTER NINE

At seven o'clock in the morning the sentry outside of the Fool's Gold Saloon was slumped in a chair and snoring. The scent of whiskey wafted from his clothes. Michael Keith emerged from the saloon and looked at Tibbs and Pap.

'They shot up the jail last night looking for you.'

'We saw that,' Tibbs said.

'Four more are inside sleeping in chairs. Hagard and about nine others are over at the Belle Union Hotel sleeping it off. It was a long night.'

'Anybody get hurt?'

'Nope. Hagard was ready to bust a seam when he realized you weren't here. He drank himself cross-eyed. Hell, they all did. None of those boys are in any shape for a gunfight today, but I reckon they're all too thick-headed to understand that. The shooting will start the moment they see you.'

'Figured as much.'

Keith looked up and down the street. He looked tired. 'I'll be glad when this is all over. Everybody will be. I am truly amazed that you are still alive.'

'Maxfield Knight will be on the train,' Tibbs said. 'When these boys wake up you tell them that.'

Keith couldn't hide his astonishment. 'Knight is coming here? I'll be damned! You're full of more tricks than a Denver dove.'

'I wouldn't know about the dove,' Tibbs said, 'but I know about Max Knight.'

They walked to the depot and stood on the platform to wait for the Union Pacific. They heard the train's whistle and finally saw a plume of smoke scratching the horizon. As the minutes ticked past they could discern the sound of the wheels rolling across the desert and the iron rails began to hum. Tibbs saw the cowcatcher reflect the sunlight as the train rounded a swell of hills and swerved into view.

The twenty ton locomotive chugged closer, wheels screeching across the rails, the smokestack belching acrid clouds into the shimmering air. When the iron behemoth rolled to a stop the air was punctured by the squeal of escaping steam and the shifting of its great iron weight as the adjoining coaches and tender car settled down like a reclining giant.

A wall of steam scrambled from the engine, momentarily obliterating the train. When the steam cleared they heard the conductor call out: 'Raven Flats!' The conductor swung himself on to the platform as the passengers began to disembark. A small, rotund businessman and his wife were first. Pap had seen the couple before. The man was a gambler and would stay only a day or two trying his luck at the late night poker tables. They were no threat. Les and Edgar Usher followed them and Pap moved to his right, putting distance between himself and Tibbs. He didn't want to make an easy target. The Usher brothers hadn't seen Tibbs yet, who stood calmly under the shingled overhang as they walked up the boardwalk toward the depot office. Both men were wearing guns.

A tall man with a handlebar mustache flecked with gray came up quickly behind them. Pap had never seen him before but he knew who he was. Maxfield Knight was dressed in a blue shirt and brown vest, his US marshal's star gleaming in the sun. The Usher brothers were oblivious to his presence. He carried a topcoat over his left arm but his right hand was free and hung loosely just inches from the walnut grip of his Colt.

Les saw Tibbs first. His eyes widened and he elbowed his brother who stared at Tibbs incredulously.

'Tibbs! You sonofabitch!' Edgar said.

Les was drawing his gun when Knight stepped up and slammed his fist into his temple. Les crumpled and with lightning speed Knight had palmed his Colt, thumbed back the hammer, and held it to Edgar's head.

'Arms up or I'll kill you.'

'What the hell is this?' Edgar put his hands in the air and stared at Knight in disbelief. Tibbs came up and pulled the gun from the now moaning Les's holster. He yanked the gun from Edgar's holster as well and held them in each hand as Les pulled himself to his feet.

'I'm US Marshal Maxfield Knight. You're both under arrest,' Knight said. 'I have warrants in my coat.'

'What's the charge? We haven't done anything wrong!'

'Embezzlement of bank funds. You'll get a chance to defend yourselves at the trial.'

'You had no right to strike me like that!' Les said.

'You can file a complaint with the judge when we get to Denver.'

82

'The jail is this way,' Tibbs said, motioning toward the sheriff's office.

'I can't believe you're still alive,' Edgar said.

'That's what people have been telling me since I got here,' Tibbs said. He nodded at Knight. 'Let's go.'

The conductor, who had observed all of this with disdain, waved at the engineer and slipped back on to the train. The train began to rumble and then suddenly it was moving again, a howling monster that slowly picked up speed as it rolled away from Raven Flats.

Pap saw a crowd of men gathering outside of the Fool's Gold Saloon as they crossed the street.

'We're gonna have company,' he said.

'I see them,' Tibbs said as they stepped on to the board-walk outside the sheriff's office. He motioned Les and Edgar through the doorway. 'You two boys are going to be real comfortable.'

Les, glancing at the bullet-riddled door and blown out window, said, 'You can't be serious!'

'Get inside.'

Once inside Tibbs locked the brothers in the cell and dropped the key in the desk drawer.

'This cell don't even have a mattress!' Edgar said.

'My father isn't going to like this,' Les said.

Knight walked up to the cell and studied the two men. They looked at him glumly, the defiance still showing in their features.

'You don't look so special,' Edgar said. 'I heard you was a tough *hombre*.'

Knight ignored him and turned back to Tibbs. 'Check the street,' he said.

Tibbs went to the door and looked out. 'It's Hagard and

five others coming this way.'

Knight looked at Pap. 'You must be Mr Wingfoot.'

'Call me Pap. I'm glad we're on the same side for this showdown.'

Knight grunted and walked out on to the boardwalk. Tibbs and Pap fanned out on each side of him. Hagard was walking toward them holding a rifle. His untucked shirt was stained with sweat and whiskey, his belt unbuckled. He looked exactly like a man that had been up all night drinking, had wakened suddenly at a loud sound, and was now attempting to piece the morning together through bleary eyes. And that, Pap thought, was probably what might get Hagard killed if he wasn't careful.

Pap recognized one of the men with Hagard as Chauncy Rawls, an angry and overweight man known for abusing women when he drank too much, which was often.

'Where's Les and Edgar?' Hagard demanded.

'Locked up inside,' Knight said. 'In two days we're taking them by train up to Denver for trial.'

'Shoot the bastard,' Chauncy said. 'That marshal star don't scare me none.'

'Shut up, Chauncy.'

'Go away,' Knight said. 'I don't have time for drunks.'

'The old man said it's a thousand dollars for him that kills Tibbs!' Chauncy exclaimed.

'I know you,' Hagard said. 'You're Max Knight. What the hell is this all about?'

'Enough of this jawin',' Chauncy said impatiently. 'Gun the bastard and let's collect that money!'

Tibbs had his eyes on Hagard but Knight kept his gaze set firmly on Chauncy. Pap took in the entire scene,

84

gauged the expressions on their faces, and knew Chauncy would draw first. Just as he had the thought Chauncy grimaced, his hand dropping for his gun, and Knight shot him in the face. The shot boomed loudly in the stillness of the hot afternoon, its echo slamming across the storefronts and spreading out into the desert like an unpleasant memory. The shot punched through Chauncy's cheek leaving a gaping hole, but Chauncy held on to his gun, his mind attempting to fathom his predicament as he swung his gun up. Another shot rang in their ears, along with the distinctive ratcheting sound of a hammer being pulled back as Knight blew Chauncy's head away. Another man, panicking, pulled his gun and Tibbs shot him in the belly. The man went down howling. All in an instant the street was filled with the coppery smell of blood, the screams of the wounded man, and four more shots from Knight's gun as he unloaded on the men. Bodies thumped to the earth and men howled in pain. Hagard dropped his rifle, his face carved in fear. He threw up his arms and screamed, 'Hold on! Hold on!'

When it was over, three men lay dead in the street and the two injured men were clutching their bloody wounds and moaning. Hagard's face was as pale as a ghost. 'Holy Jesus!' he muttered.

Pap watched Knight flip open the Colt's loading gate and punch out the empty shells. His hand worked swiftly as he pulled cartridges from his belt loops and reloaded the gun. Pap had never seen anyone reload a Colt single-action army revolver with such assurance and he knew he was in the presence of greatness.

Knight leveled his steely gaze on Hagard. 'Bury the dead and get the wounded to a doctor. That train comes

85

back heading north in two days. If I see you before then I'll shoot you on sight. If Carleton Usher wants to see his sons he can visit them in the Denver jail.' Knight looked at Pap. 'Keep an eye on things out here awhile.' Pap nodded and set himself in the chair, shotgun across his knees. Knight and Tibbs holstered their guns and went into the jail, shutting the bullet riddled door behind them.

Yep, just like Bull Run! Pap thought. And now the vultures will feed.

Wallace Gip, the undertaker, appeared with several men who helped him carry away the dead. Hagard and the wounded slinked away. None of them looked at Pap. The day was incredibly hot and silent. The boardwalks were empty, although Pap noticed that Micheal Keith emerged from his saloon once to look up and down the street. Jamie's store was quiet. Fifteen minutes later he saw the Mexican, Feliciano, on horseback at the far western edge of the street. Then the Mexican disappeared and all was silent.

He could hear Tibbs and Knight talking inside but he couldn't make out their words. Then the blackbirds dropped silently from the air like specters and began pecking at the scraps of Chauncy's brains that lay splattered across the dusty street like bloody cauliflower.

Hot damn! thought Pap. Knight and Tibbs can't really believe they'll get the Usher brothers on to that train. No siree! This showdown isn't anywhere near being finished yet!

CHAPTER TEN

'He's a deputy US marshal?'

Carleton Usher couldn't believe what he was hearing.

'And Max Knight is with him. They got Les and Edgar locked up in jail.'

Hagard felt a hollowness in his belly as he looked at the old man. His face, wrinkled from both age and perhaps his own evil nature, stared contemptuously at him as he delivered the news. The room was stifling hot – Hagard wondered how the old man could stand being closed in a dark room all day in this heat – and it smelled of body odor, tobacco smoke, and something else. There was a scent that he couldn't identify, but as he stood there looking at the old man he thought the scent reminded him of death. Yes, that was it. The old man was dying. Death oozed from his pores like a perfume. Hagard took a step back.

'What's wrong with you?' Usher said. 'Don't you step back from me!'

'I'm just tired is all.'

'You've been drinking. All those men were drinking weren't they?'

'There was nothin' else to do after Tibbs got away last night.'

'I should shoot you myself. Robert E. Lee would have hung you out to dry for your foolishness.'

'He's got that damn marshal with him now. . . .'

'Max Knight. The Yankee lawman that marched with General Sherman. They write dime novels about murderers like him. Now you listen to me so we can end this. Wasn't that Hart girl sweet on Tibbs all those years ago? You fetch her here. Don't hurt her and don't let anyone see you.' Usher pulled an old Navy Colt from his mahogany desk drawer. He set the gun on the desk. 'After you fetch the girl send Feliciano to Tibbs with an ultimatum. My boys or the girl dies. I'll shoot the bitch myself.'

'You want me to take some of the boys with me?'

'Go alone, you damn fool. If you get killed it's your own damn fault. If you don't do what I ask I'll personally hunt you down.' Usher picked up the gun, his eyes blazing.

Hagard left the room, the sight of his broken nose and purpled face too much for Usher to bear. He was incompetent. Let Tibbs kill him. Usher would finish this himself. He poured himself a glass of bourbon and tipped it down his throat. The cobwebs dissipated and his stomach boiled. He sat down in his leather chair and examined the Navy Colt. Hagard was a fool – the gun wasn't loaded. Usher pulled a cigar box from his desk and inside he found a scattering of percussion caps, a tin of gunpowder, the 36 caliber lead balls, and pinchers to affix the caps. He pressed the caps on to all six cylinder nipples and poured gunpowder into the cylinder before pressing the lead balls in with the loading rammer.

He remembered the first Union soldier he'd killed with this gun all those years past. A line of gun caissons pulled by a team of quarter horses breathing steam into the cold October air clopped past and a boy with ruffled hair was brought forward. His blue shirt had been torn from his frame and he stood shivering in his white undershirt and torn blue pants. They had removed his boots and his pale, bare feet were flecked with mud. He asked the boy where the Union officers were camped and the boy said, 'I dunno, sir' between shivering teeth. Usher shot him in the head and instructed the men to leave his body in the road as a warning to the Yankee filth that had destroyed his home. . . .

The old man went out of the room and down the hall to Pete's room. His son was reclining on a bed, light streaming through the open window. The old man squinted against the light. Pete tried to sit up in bed. The sight of his father had startled him. The old man looked at the bandaged leg.

'Can you ride?'

'It hurts, Pa, you know that it's gotta hurt.'

'I didn't ask you if it hurt. I asked if you could ride.'

His tone was as hollow as the wind through a cemetery.

'Pa, it hurts bad. I might be able to ride, but not far.'

'You'll ride then. When the time comes I'll have your horse and gun ready.'

'What are we going to do?'

The old man had turned to flee the scathing sunlight but paused and stared at his son. Under the glare of the sun the veins beneath his skin squirmed like pale purple

89

worms, his eyes tearing in the yellow light.

'We're going to kill people,' he said, 'We're going to rally the boys and kill the enemy.' He went quickly from the room, his footsteps echoing down the hall. Pete Usher breathed a heavy sigh.

Carleton Usher returned to his dark room to sit at his desk and plan the murder of Cole Tibbs and Maxfield Knight just as he had the evening he decided to have Reginald Tibbs killed. But the sight of his son Pete reclining on the bed with his bloody leg kept intruding on his thoughts. He tried to recall the faces of his sons' mothers. They were lost to him, and while he didn't care, he discovered that he was curious if his sons all carried too much of their mothers' personalities. Pete was the weakest, Sam had been the dumbest. There was hope for Les and Edgar but even those two fools had allowed themselves to be taken prisoner.

He poured another glass of bourbon and swallowed it in one gulp. Rally the boys, he thought, show them how to fight like men.

He removed his coat and draped it over a chair. His white shirt was damp with perspiration and he smelled his own fecund body odor. Another glass of bourbon disappeared. He began to nod off and his mind was filled suddenly with a long suppressed memory that wafted across his senses like a woman's perfume. He recalled a time five years after the war when he thought he might actually find happiness. He had met a woman named Veronica with long black hair and flashing eyes. They spent a week together in San Antonio and the days were all golden warmth and tempestuous nights; long walks along the riverbank and the scent of chicken and potato

90

lunches in the tall grass. Then one month later she had taken his money belt and fled town on a stagecoach. The hotel clerk eventually told him she was a whore from Chicago and that the tall man he'd seen her talking with was her partner. So once again a northerner had taken something from him. He caught up with Veronica and her man in Galveston where he made them walk out into the surf of a bitterly cold Gulf of Mexico and swim for their lives. 'All the way to Florida!' he had told them, waving his Navy Colt. 'You might make it!' Their bodies washed ashore three days later. The sharks had torn open their torsos.

Usher understood all too well that his had been an unhappy life, filled with deceit, betrayal and murder. He was no fool. He had supplanted happiness with power and financial success. No woman had ever loved him; his own sons feared him; the men he'd killed haunted his slumber. He was alone in his room but the room was crowded with every man that had died by his hand. The gunshots echoed across time.

Of late he had dreamed of a tall man in black riding toward him. He couldn't see the man's face. As the man rode closer he could discern the navy blue hat and gold braid. So it was a Union soldier coming to exact a vengeance against him.

Maxfield Knight?

He opened his eyes. How long had he dreamed? He stood up and walked out on to the porch of the home that had once belonged to Reginald Tibbs. It was late afternoon and the sun burned the land a deep, rich brown.

Rally them, boys!

He shrugged his memories aside and sat in his rocking

91

chair to wait. A short time later Feliciano walked out of the bunkhouse and approached him.

'Two riders are coming. Señor Hagard and another.'

'Sit down and wait with me.'

Feliciano pulled up a chair without comment and waited. Presently Hagard rode in trailing a mule by a rope. Astride the mule sat Jamie Hart, gagged and tied. Her eyes flashed furiously when she saw the men on the porch. Hagard dismounted and pulled Jamie from the saddle, pushing her toward the porch.

'Did anyone see you?' Usher asked.

'No, Tibbs and Knight are inside the sheriff's office. Pap Wingfoot is sitting outside with a shotgun. I went in the back and they never saw me.'

Usher studied Jamie. 'Listen to me, girl,' he began. 'I will have one of the women remove your gag later. You will stay in the bunkhouse with Conchita.' Then turning to Feliciano he added, 'Have Ramon outside with a rifle. If she tries to escape kill her.'

Tears welled in Jamie's eyes. 'Don't start that weeping,' Usher said, 'or I'll have you shot now. If you do as you're told I'll release you afterward. Meanwhile, you are a prisoner of war.' He nodded to Feliciano. 'Take her to Conchita. Then take Hagard here and José to town. From this moment on I want someone watching Tibbs and Knight around the clock. Keep José ready with a horse to ride back and report to me. I want every man ready to ride with his guns loaded when I give the word.' Usher pointed at Hagard. 'You tell them we have the girl and I'm proposing a swap. Her life for the release of my sons. They have three days and then I'll kill her myself.'

Hagard didn't like it. 'They might shoot me when I tell

them about the girl! Those men are dangerous.'

Usher's eyes burned with an unholy fire. 'They're not as dangerous as I am. Go!'

CHAPTER ELEVEN

Pap Wingfoot saw Hagard, Feliciano, and José turn their mounts on to Main Street. They tethered their horses at the hitching rail outside the Fool's Gold Saloon and looked up the street at Pap. Pap rose to his feet and without taking his eyes from the three men his right hand swung down and back and rapped on the office door as a signal. The three men began making their way slowly down the street.

Tibbs and Knight emerged from the office and stood with Pap on the boardwalk. Hagard looked as miserable as he felt but Pap didn't like the shine in his eyes. Hagard held his hands out.

'You can see that I don't have a gun in my hand,' he said.

'But you wear one in your holster,' Tibbs replied.

'I'm not drawing my gun. I came here to offer information. You need to hear this.'

The two Mexicans stood silently at Hagard's side as he spoke. It was obvious they posed no threat, but Pap wondered if it was obvious to Hagard. Probably not. They were Usher's men and Usher demanded loyalty. But Pap had

94

known Feliciano since he was a boy, and Tibbs had known him, too. Feliciano wouldn't pull his gun, and neither would José.

'Get to it,' Tibbs said.

'The old man has Miss Hart. Says he's gonna kill her if you don't swap for Les and Edgar.'

Tibbs was off the boardwalk, his hands at Hagard's throat. Hagard went to his knees choking as Knight came up and yanked Tibbs loose.

'Not now.'

Hagard spit into the dust, his face red. 'You had no call to choke me!'

'You're lucky I don't kill you now,' Tibbs hissed.

'I'm delivering a message is all,' Hagard gasped. 'I ain't pulled my gun, damn you!'

Knight stepped between the two men. 'Where's the old man now?' he asked.

'At the house. He's got all the men ready to ride against you boys. You ain't got a chance.'

'We'll see about that.'

'You got three days and then he'll shoot that girl. He'll do it, too. You don't know him. You don't know what he's capable of.'

'Oh yes I do,' Knight said. 'I rode against southern boys like him before. I think it's time I had a talk with Mr Usher.' He looked at Tibbs. 'I know what you're thinking, but stay here. I'll be back before sundown.'

Tibbs nodded. 'The house is a few miles up the road past the creek. You'll find it easily enough.'

Knight gestured at Hagard. 'Lock him up. I'm taking his horse.' Looking at Feliciano he said, 'You'll ride with me to the Usher ranch.'

'*Sí*, señor.'

'You can't lock me up without a reason!' Hagard protested, but before he could say another word Knight slammed a rock-hard fist into his jaw. Hagard's eyes rolled and he crumpled. Pap chuckled.

Feliciano followed Knight and they untied the horses and began the trek to the ranch. Knight looked back and saw Tibbs and Pap hauling Hagard into the jail. He knew what Tibbs must be going through but he was proud of his discipline. He was following orders without an argument. It had to be eating him up, but he had remained fairly calm. Their best chance of saving Miss Hart lay in their ability to work through the situation calmly and logically, although they both knew it wouldn't be easy.

Tibbs had told him that Feliciano and the Mexicans would remain neutral, but had to appear as if they followed Usher's orders. With this in mind he said to Feliciano as they rode from town, 'There's less chance the other men will fire when I ride in with you. Hand me your gun and you'll be under my jurisdiction until I leave.' Feliciano nodded and handed over his gun.

Knight was otherwise lost in his thoughts as they rode. He thought about the cold, barren fields outside of Atlanta all those years ago, and the stark look of desolation in the displaced people whose lives had been destroyed by a war of opposing ideologies. And he thought about the years afterward as a lawman, always encountering that war again in different forms, and the rioting confusion that his life had become at times.

He realized that he was riding again to face the same enemy. The name was different, but the scolding look of hatred would be familiar to him. A grisly parade of dead

96

enemies trooped through his mind and he wondered if all men that experienced war were haunted by the past. Surely Usher had heard of him. What must he think to realize his old enemy rides toward him yet again and with the same solemn purpose?

They came upon Snakebite Creek and Feliciano took the lead.

'Be careful, *señor*. There are many rattlesnakes.'

They crossed a rocky plateau and Knight saw several snakes lazing in the sun, their black and gold triangular markings all too familiar to the lawman. The dry rattle from their tails suddenly filled the air with its bristling sound. Their horses flicked their ears nervously. They passed the rocks and on to a short embankment before crossing the creek. Emerging from the water they found themselves again traversing a rocky area where more snakes lie curled on the rocks to warm their cold-blooded souls. Despite the heat, Knight shivered.

He breathed a sigh of relief when they rode into the desert following the trail to Usher's ranch. After a few minutes he could see the sprawling house in the distance. When they crossed the fence line and swung on to the main property there was a lot of activity around the bunkhouse on their left. A dozen men appeared with rifles, including a few Mexicans. Carleton Usher was standing on the porch watching them ride in. Knight noticed he had an old Navy Colt in a holster on his hip.

Goddamn, Knight thought, *he looks like an undertaker!*

They rode right up to the porch but remained astride their horses.

'I'm US Marshal Maxfield Knight.'

'I know who you are.'

'I understand you are holding a woman named Jamie Hart against her will.'

'I can have you shot out of your saddle, sir. But I am not a murderer like you heathen Yankees. You can ride out before I forget my manners.'

Knight looked up at the sky. He glanced over at the riflemen near the bunkhouse, and then he looked at the house. He finally looked down at Usher. The skinny old man was sweating profusely. His skin was incredibly white and Knight wondered if he was partly an albino. His sunken cheekbones gave him a cadaverous look. The only real sign of life in Carleton Usher lay in his hot, dark eyes. They blazed at Knight and he could feel the hatred as strongly as if he were being pushed.

'I asked you about a woman.'

'What did you hope to accomplish by coming here? Your life is in my hands. I had not heard that the famous Max Knight was a fool.'

'I came here to look at you,' Knight said.

Usher was surprised. 'And now you have seen me.'

'I like to know something about a man if I have to kill him.'

Usher's hand almost went for his Colt but Knight held his gaze and the old man flinched. 'I've done nothing to you. But you Yankees marched through Atlanta destroying everything in sight. Explain yourself, sir.'

'I want Miss Jamie Hart released unharmed. If that doesn't happen I'm coming back here and I'll kill you. Your sons are under arrest and will stand trial in Denver on embezzlement charges.'

'My attorney will have those charges dropped. Mr Cole Tibbs fabricated those charges to suit his purpose. His father was a poor gambler. No jury will convict my sons when they learn the deputy that arrested them lost his family home because his father bet the deed in a poker game.'

Knight rubbed his jaw with his hand and looked off into the distance. Feliciano had not moved in all the time Knight and Usher had been speaking. Now he glanced at Knight.

'Mr Usher, you and I can sit here all day and fight the war again, but the outcome will be the same. I want you to think on what I've said. The woman needs to be released or I can't guarantee your sons will live to see Denver.'

Usher started forward, a curse flinging from his lips, but something in Knight's gaze stopped him. Knight reined his horse around and began riding out, Feliciano beside him. When they had reached the gate he glanced back and Usher stood like a statue glaring at him, his dark eyes the only sign of life in his slender, pale form.

CHAPTER TWELVE

Feliciano told Knight the old man would order an attack. 'Maybe tonight, *señor*. I have seen him angry like this.'

Knight nodded but said nothing. Once again they crossed Snakebite Creek and Knight reined his horse to a halt.

'This is where Reginald Tibbs was murdered?'

'*Sí*, señor.'

'Tell me what you know.'

'The old man wanted to buy *señor* Tibbs out. He refused. Mr Tibbs and the old man played cards. One night they said his son was hurt and to come with them. They killed him here. Mr Cole was drunk, *señor*. A young man drinks too much sometimes.'

Knight frowned. 'Well, he's not drunk now.'

'No, *señor*. He fights good.'

They rode on past the harsh rattle of Snakebite Creek, the sun beating on their backs. Knight had learned enough and he felt prepared. Usher would certainly attack them now. He'd seen it in the old man's eyes.

After giving Feliciano his gun back, Knight tied Hagard's horse at the hitching rail outside of the Fool's

100

Gold Saloon. Feliciano was joined by José and they chose to wait out the afternoon inside the saloon. Knight left them to their jugs of warm beer and found Tibbs sitting at the desk inside the jail. He told Tibbs what had happened and that he expected a retaliation.

'The old man won't wait three days.'

'We'll have our hands full if it's a dozen or more. There's not much of a defense here,' Tibbs said.

Knight thought it over. 'He'll use the same tactics as Lee or Grant. He'll send skirmishers to flank us. He'll expect that might be the end of it. He has a picket line at the ranch and he might set up a line around town. He knows you slipped past him once already.'

'The picket line is the key,' Pap said.

'How so?' Tibbs asked.

'The pickets, or what they call the *videttes*, can prevent our escape and result in our deaths. The *videttes* serve as a warning signal and can often turn the tide in battle.'

'I know a place where we can hide,' Tibbs said, 'But taking three prisoners causes an additional problem.'

'Two prisoners. We have to let Hagard go.'

'We'll end up regretting that later.'

'Then we'll kill him later,' Knight said, 'but he's not coming with us.'

'We'll need a diversion,' Pap said.

Knight looked at him but remained silent.

'All right, I'm the diversion,' Pap continued. 'You and Cole take them out of town. I'll keep them guessing a while.'

'Arguing with him won't do any good,' Tibbs said to Knight.

'I figured as much. We have our work cut out for us.'

Knight motioned to the adjoining jail room door and Tibbs picked up the brass key ring, opened the door and entered the cellblock where the three prisoners stared at them glumly from behind bars.

'You gonna let us go?' Edgar asked.

Tibbs unlocked the cell. 'Hagard, get up.'

Hagard walked out of the cell and Knight gestured for him to stop in the sheriff's office. Tibbs locked the cell again and ignored the stream of profanity that Les and Edgar sent flying his way.

'I'll take my gunbelt,' Hagard said to Tibbs.

'Not today,' Knight said. 'Get going.'

Hagard looked at Knight and then turned and strode from the office. Pap whistled softly between his teeth.

'He's got a bad look in his eyes.'

'Next time we see him we'll shoot him,' Knight said.

'Now we wait awhile,' Tibbs said.

'We'll wait. I have to think this over. It's a few hours before sundown yet.'

Knight went out leaving Tibbs in the office and Pap once again posted in his chair on the boardwalk. When he glanced out at the horizon he saw a mass of purple clouds climbing into the sky. A mountain of gray and purple rose in the northwest like a demon awakening from a slumber. But the sky overhead was still eggshell blue and shimmering with heat. The sun still beat down mercilessly. His shirt was damp with sweat.

The coming desert storm gave him reason to pause. Knight didn't like the set-up. Their position in town was defensible, but at what cost? How many would die? For Knight, it wasn't a matter of surviving, it was a matter of killing – Usher's men would wither under the bark of his

102

Colt. He didn't like the plan of hiding near Snakebite Creek. He had seen the area and their defenses were minimal. One man could hide out easily enough, but two men and two prisoners made it suicidal.

They could avoid the picket line well enough but eventually Usher's men would find them. They had to be in town to catch that train.

But could they use the storm to their advantage?

He thought it through from every angle and assessed the possibilities.

He stood on the boardwalk outside of the Fool's Gold Saloon and looked up the street at the sheriff's office. He studied the buildings; their height, access to rooftops, alleyways, sheds, outhouses, and utility shacks. He made a mental picture of the town's layout.

The scent of the air had changed: Knight could smell the rain. The far horizon was jumbled with thick clouds that pulsed with lightning. The storm was moving quickly across the desert.

He made up his mind and strode quickly to the sheriff's office where he found Tibbs at the desk playing solitaire. Pap followed Knight into the office. He told them his plan. When he was finished Tibbs looked at him and nodded.

'There has to be one change,' Tibbs said.

'What's that?'

'I have to be the one that goes after Jamie. I know the land better. I grew up here and I can make my way across that desert in the dark or blindfolded. With that storm coming you might get disoriented.'

Knight reluctantly agreed. 'Pap and I will set up our own line of defense.'

103

Thirty minutes later the sky turned gray and the flickering mass of thunderclouds seemed poised at the edge of the world. The northwestern sky was completely obliterated by peaks of nearly black clouds, the lightning crackling among its ridges and valleys like an angry behemoth.

The air become deathly still and Grant, Pap's yellow dog, crawled under the boardwalk.

The blackbirds that usually occupied the dusty street were gone.

Hell was about to descend on Raven Flats.

CHAPTER THIRTEEN

Cole Tibbs made his way across the desert as the storm broke. The sand flowed into a strand of thorny mesquite where he stopped, his right hand on his holstered Colt. Under his left arm he carried a rolled canvas awning cut from the frame of an old wagon. The sun had vanished into a boiling mass of thunderclouds. Cold rain had begun to splatter against the desert which greedily soaked up the raindrops. His visibility was limited and growing worse by the minute as the unseen sun sank below the distant mountains.

The deceptive desert landscape required his diligence. At a glance the path may appear level but the desert is rife with swales and gullies where a man might easily stumble. A thirty foot drop in a gully could foretell a man's doom. The southwest had seen the bones of many lost travelers bleached to white ash under the blistering sun. But Tibbs knew his way and walked confidently through a stygian blackness that would have given the stoutest of men reason to tremble.

He was a hundred yards from the perimeter of Snakebite Creek when he heard the riders. The clip-clop of hoof beats splashed across the creek and Tibbs tried to count horses but the darkness was too thick. But judging from the hoof beats he estimated at least ten riders, maybe more. By the time the riders had crossed the creek the rain was beating down steadily, the air now cold.

When he was satisfied that the riders had passed he proceeded into the rocky swell that bordered Snakebite Creek. The rain began to lash fiercely and Tibbs made his way by instinct through the swirling darkness.

The first peals of thunder shattered the night and sent echoes rolling across the desert like the memory of artillery fire. In the lightning flash that followed Tibbs saw snakes wriggling furiously across the rocks, their diamondback markings undulating as the sidewinders sought shelter. A shiver ran down his spine.

He stopped and struck his boot heel upon the rocks several times. The reverberation should scatter any snakes in his path. But he couldn't be certain. The storm had agitated the wildlife. In the next lightning flash he witnessed a snake chomping its jaws on to a jack rabbit that had flown across its path. Immersed in a terrific struggle the snake whipped out on the rocks, and with each successive flash of lightning the rabbit's struggle lessened as its body was forced past the rattlesnake's fang-gleaming jaws. The snake constricted until the rabbit's body was a bulge at its center.

He swept past the snake and crossed a large boulder where he paused again. When the lightning flashed he noted that his former hiding place was free of snakes or animals and he slid down the incline where he left the rolled canvas next his saddle-bag.

When the lightning flashed the rocks looked to be

bruised and bloody, the craggy crevices resembled faces peering at him from beneath the winking splinter of lightning. The stark squirm of a diamondback rattlesnake slithering across a boulder as the wind echoed the sound of gunfire from Raven Flats turned the night into a grotesque nightmare played out in pantomime.

Knight and Pap had their hands full now. Tibbs could hear the boom of Pap's shotgun followed by the bark of a Colt. Men were dying in the night, their spirits sent heavenward by thundering lead as nature seemed to offer its own protest against the violent actions of men.

With the canvas resting next to his saddle-bag he made his way out of the hollow depression and climbed again over the rocks to make his way to the creek. Amid the tumult of wind and thunder he could hear Snakebite Creek trickling along with a steady pulse that belied the stark heat-blasted landscape that had cost so many men their lives. The storm was a welcome respite, but equally as deadly as the blistering sun. Tibbs knew to avoid trees which often suffered the ravages of a lightning strike.

The creek was shallow, barely exceeding his ankles, and he entered the adjoining grassy swell where he knew snakes thrived. A sense of urgency propelled him through the grass as he heard Pap's shotgun boom again in the dark distance behind him. When he heard a rattle a moment later he stopped and waited for a lightning flash to show him the way. He went quickly and breathed a sigh of relief when his boots struck sand and he found himself within inches of a prickly pear cactus.

The blackness had swallowed him.

The house where he had grown up was invisible against

the black wall that blocked his way. The wind began to scream and the rain was cold and furious. He pulled his Stetson down over his eyes and trudged onward.

He was making his way by memory and instinct. The minutes passed with unbearable slowness. His clothes were soaked and he felt a slight chill. He moved slowly, cautiously, for experience had shown him the desert was twice as deadly during an electrical storm than when the sun beat down like molten iron.

His legs ached from their exertions. When his hand brushed against his Colt the walnut grip was cold and slick with rain. His clothes clung to him like chilly leeches. Minutes stretched into eternity and he began to feel the weight of exhaustion begin to nip at his heels.

Then he came upon a fence-post by crashing into it.

He knew where he was.

He was standing at the corral fence line not fifty feet from the bunkhouse where Feliciano had said Jamie was being held. On a moonless night he would have seen the oil lamps glittering beyond the thin veil of curtain but the storm had reduced his visibility to zero.

He followed the fence-line, turned the corner, and came up against the bunkhouse. Only the rain-chilled wind greeted him as he gazed into the swirling darkness.

A sudden burst of thunder cracked open the heavens followed by a crackling snake of lightning that turned the night into an electric inferno. Somewhere he heard cursing in Spanish. Tibbs knew a little Spanish.

God is angry, a voice said, followed by a curse. *The Devil walks tonight!*

He went to the door and listened.

Voices inside, but none that he recognized. How many

guards were posted inside? One? Two? He had to make a decision soon.

He pulled his Colt and took a breath.

There's no time like now, he thought, as he pushed open the door and stepped inside.

Conchita was sitting at a table with two small Mexican boys. The old man with her he remembered, too. Pablo. They looked at him in amazement but said nothing. Tibbs glanced about the room. No guards.

'Where is she?' he rasped.

'*Madre de Dios!* He has taken her, *señor.* To the house they go!' Conchita held rosary beads between her shaking hands. They looked at the gun in his hand.

Tibbs nodded, turned and stepped out into the lashing rain. As the lightning flashed, the house where he had been raised loomed like a dark and foreboding fortress against the tumultuous night sky. The wind pummeled him as he traversed the space between the bunkhouse and the front porch, a sound like screeching ravens filled his ears.

Tibbs wasted no time. He was on to the porch and quickly pushed open the door. He entered the house with his thumb poised over the Colt's hammer.

CHAPTER
FOURTEEN

Maxfield Knight heard the boom of Pap's shotgun followed by the painful wail of a man with his legs blown apart. A minute later a lightning flash revealed the man slumped in the street, his gun in the dirt, his body twitching as he bled to death.

Knight had positioned himself across from the jail while Pap had taken up residence on the boardwalk behind two flour barrels. A horse trough provided additional cover. Hagard had ridden into town with a dozen men an hour earlier just as the storm had struck. The Usher brothers were locked in their cells and Knight and Pap had nailed the rear entrance door closed and barricaded it with the sheriff's old desk. The front entrance was unlocked but Pap had set three chairs before the door and then propped several rusty tin cans on to the chairs. Anyone near that doorway would make noise resulting in a blast of hot lead from Pap's shotgun.

From his position in the darkened doorway across from the jail he could move easily up and down the boardwalk to fire upon Hagard's men when they closed in. Anyone approaching the jail would be caught in a crossfire angled in such a way that neither Knight nor Pap were in danger of shooting each other. They had a full view of the street.

But Knight knew nothing would be easy. Some of these men were hardened, soulless killers.

Michael Keith had shuttered The Fool's Gold Saloon but Hagard and his men had quickly retreated to the hotel half a block away.

The wind came in with a harsh torrent of rain and the tin cans Pap had carefully placed on the chairs went clattering into the dark. They would have to listen for the scuttle-sound of chairs being swept aside and that might be impossible above the howl of the thunderstorm that crouched in the heavens above them like a snarling beast.

Two bodies lay in the street. One had fallen under the muzzle of Knight's Colt; the other had been torn to bits just moments ago by Pap's shotgun.

Pap had said the odds were against them but Knight disagreed. Knight had no qualms about killing when there was no choice. He had known about killing for a very long time. When the time came he would kill quickly and ruthlessly, whatever emotion that he felt buried in a dark place in his soul.

Several months past he had been obligated to hunt down a half-breed killer that had been robbing stages outside of Deadwood. During the course of his investigation he had learned of certain personal matters that convinced him this man had been given an unfair chance in life, but he was still a killer. And when they finally faced each other Knight had swallowed his emotions yet again and walked away from the man's corpse.

For a long while there was nothing for him to do but hunker down in the doorway and let the storm rage. None of them was any match for nature's fury and as the lightning crackled and the thunder boomed Knight glared out into the dark street determined that his mission would be completed satisfactorily. A US marshal shared with the Texas Rangers the distinction of being men that refused to quit. There would be no negotiations.

So far none of Usher's men had demonstrated any talent for fighting. Knight had been fighting battles of one type or another for a long time. Sometimes those memories intruded on his thoughts with the stinging ferocity of a wasp. . . .

He was awakened one morning by the crowing of a rooster. They were just miles from Savannah and before he could finish his breakfast of cold rice and poor beef an artillery shell screamed through the air and exploded twenty feet from the sentry. The shrapnel shattered the sentry's musket and tore off his arm at the elbow before ripping through his belly. By the time Knight and four others had reached his side the sentry's eyes stared fixedly at the sky where clouds floated past on a breeze that smelled of gunpowder. The mercury, Knight was told later, would reach sixty degrees that day. They were only ten miles from Savannah and among the ranks it was believed victory could only be postponed but not forfeited by anything the rebels threw at them. But a man in battle doesn't think about such things. He only thinks about survival. He thinks about killing the man in front of him and killing the man behind that man. General Sherman had accepted that by sheer force of stomping the serpent his twisting spine will eventually break. Stomp the goddamn serpent, boys!

Knight stared into the blackness. His memories faded like the echo of gunfire.

Old man Usher had sent a dozen men to kill him and Pap and only a few skirmishers had shown themselves.

They were being tested. But for what purpose?

Usher was a tactician as are all military commanders. But Hagard possessed no skill and but a flicker of intelligence, which made him all the more dangerous. Hired guns like Hagard didn't think about tactics, they thought about getting the job done as quickly as possible. The waves of wind and rain slashed across the town and the rain spooled from his hat brim where the wind threw it into the darkness like shattered glass.

He detected movement in the dark.

At least two men had quietly slipped out of the hotel and were making their way slowly down the boardwalk. Knight sensed them more than saw them. They would cross in front of him.

A sliver of yellow light blinked again and he knew two more men had emerged from the hotel. But they moved right, away from Knight.

They wanted to flank him, box him in.

Or distract him. Or both.

Knight reacted instantly, his gun in hand, and stepped into the street preparing to engage the closest two men. But when the lightning flashed the street was empty.

Stunned, he stepped back, moved up the boardwalk to a position almost directly opposite the jail.

They would have gone between the buildings to make their way behind the jail.

A useless move, thought Knight. The rear entrance was solidly barricaded and any effort to breech the door would bring Pap with his shotgun.

He felt a presence in the darkness. Nearby on his right,

somewhere in that wall of darkness where the second duo had disappeared, something had moved. A spur jingled.

Then the stars burst free behind his eyes and the air was knocked from his lungs as the two men stumbled into him. They immediately lashed out with their fists and Knight cursed himself for being caught by surprise. Knight struck one man so hard in the stomach that his fist felt as if it had disappeared into his flesh. Then he slammed another fist into the man's ribs and he heard the ribs shatter with a painful crack. The man grunted and went down. With practiced speed Knight's Colt was flung into his hand and the darkness was blown away by the thundering blast of his .45 as he shot the other man in the chest. The shot blew the man from the boardwalk and he flopped into the muddy street with his arms outstretched, the rain painting his face with an unwelcome penitence.

Pap's shotgun boomed across the street.

As if Mother Nature had planned the scene, Knight felt the wind and rain die down as the storm subsided, at least temporarily, and the cool night air felt good on his face. A dark figure loomed before him as his assailant pulled himself to his feet with a grunt. Knight slammed two quick punches into him; one to his already cracked ribs followed by a haymaker to his head. The man yelped and went down, unconscious. Knight yanked the man's gun from its holster and dropped it into a horse trough.

He found Pap a few moments later across the street.

'You hit anything?'

'Not that time. Two of them came up the boardwalk and disappeared.'

'There's an injured man over there, but I think he's finished.'

'Plenty left where he came from.'

'Stay hidden,' Knight said, and then he walked away.

'I've got that part figured out,' Pap grumbled to himself. 'And kill any bad-asses that come my way. Nothin' to it.'

Knight disappeared into the darkness just as a breeze tainted by rain and smelling of decay swept across his face. As he strode on to the boardwalk two things happened. First there came the sound of spurs rattling nearby and Knight froze. Someone stood very near him in the dark, perhaps twenty feet away. The man was standing in the street but positioned near the boardwalk. He was standing near the six inch wood post that braced the shingled over-hang that shaded this section of boardwalk. Knight could smell the whiskey even at this distance. Some men never learn and die the hard way.

The second was the ominous click of a Colt's hammer being pulled back as the man lifted his gun.

Most men would have fled, crouched, whimpered in fear, and probably died. But Maxfield Knight was unlike most men. He was an avenging angel, implacable and far more dangerous than the man he faced. His Colt bucked in his hand, flame spewing from the barrel, the lead blast-ing a hole into his adversary's chest. As the man was dropping lifelessly to the ground he heard yet another click, this time on his right, and a man in the alley died just as quickly, as Knight's Colt blazed again, his first shot still echoing off the storefronts. A man grunted and fell.

Gunsmoke hung in the air. The gunshots had torn open the night's stillness. Lightning flashed in the amber heavens and he heard the distant rumble of thunder. This storm, and the one boiling in the sky, would not recede until more men had been sent on their way to hell.

'Bring it on, you bastards!' Knight said to the darkness.

A boot scuffed against the boardwalk and Knight spun, fired, and moved to another position. His shot had missed, but it didn't matter. He walked slowly, methodically, his senses alert for any sound, any movement. His eyes swept the darkness, probed the veil of blackness, and discerned shapes. He instinctively assessed those shapes, judged their potential for danger, all while walking slowly and silently to a position on the boardwalk closer to the hotel. He wanted a better view of the hotel's doorway.

A door creaked open. Another yellow sliver of light poured into the darkness and just as quickly disappeared. A raspy voice said: 'The rain's stopped.' And nearby another voice said: 'You got the matches?'

Dark figures moved up the street, away from the jail.

They were leading him on. But as Knight had the thought he changed his mind. His eyes had adjusted to the darkness and he saw the two men slip into an alley. There was nothing back there but desert. Why would they go behind the buildings?

He walked across the street and stepped on to the boardwalk. He walked toward the jail and when he came to a space between the buildings he stopped and listened.

Voices. The two men were approaching the jail from the rear.

You got the matches?

They couldn't be serious about trying to burn the building down. It was suicide. Pap and Knight would be on to them and even with dry matches the wet wood would take time to burn. He tried to fathom what instructions Usher had given them. What would he do? He went down the

116

alley, gun in hand, and came out behind the Dry Goods store. He was less than thirty seconds behind the two men. They would be behind the jail but all was silent.

He heard scuffling in the dark, followed by a curse.

'Goddamn it! Don't drop the matches!'

'All right, you old cowpuncher.'

And in that instant Knight realized their only option and he bellowed 'Hold it!' But it was too late. A wooden match struck against a cocked boot-heel and flared to life. The wick on the dynamite stick sizzled like an Independence Day firecracker and the dynamite was tossed against the adobe wall of the jail. Knight's gun roared, his bullet slamming into a wall to no avail. He heard the two men running.

The blast knocked him to the ground.

Pap's shotgun boomed once, then a second time.

Out in the street a group of men let out jubilant yells.

Yee-haw!

Busted adobe, dust, and dirt rained down around Knight. His ears were humming with the repercussion. He pulled himself to his feet as footsteps receded into the darkness. Pap's shotgun boomed again and then he was running. Turning the corner he saw dark figures in the street. He fired, his Colt bucking angrily in his hand.

Pap was pinned down on the boardwalk with the horse trough and a barrel of flour for cover. Knight fired again and a man yowled in pain. He took a breath, his heart hammering in his chest. His Colt spat flame and hot lead. Unseen men screamed in agony, falling into the street to die alone, unseen in the dark. The moment was reduced to Knight's speed with a six-shooter and his unerring senses. With his Colt empty he flipped open the loading gate and punched out the spent shells. The brass was hot as it was flung aside. And in an instant he thumbed fresh cartridges into the cylinder and snapped shut the loading gate.

A man rushed him in the dark, fists flailing, and he was knocked to the ground. His Colt spun out of his hand. From a prone position he struck out with his boot and caught the man on the thigh. Knight rolled and sprung to his feet. He immediately threw a hard right and caught the man a grazing blow on the jaw. But now Knight had his distance. He slammed three fast punches into the man's head and followed with an uppercut to the stomach. The man grunted as the air burst from his lungs and Knight jacked his balled fist into the man's head, knocking him unconscious.

The night exploded with gunfire. Bullets whizzed in the air and thumped into the street or along the boardwalk. Pap's shotgun boomed again and another man screamed as his body crumpled in the darkness. Knight flung himself into the dirt and began crawling, his mind alive with the memory of just such a moment all those years ago when the Johnny Rebs opened up with artillery fire. There was no shame in crawling, not as long as a man got up again. Knight reached the boardwalk and called out hoarsely 'Pap!'

'Up here, Marshal!'

Pap's shotgun tore a hole in the fabric of darkness, the blast shaking the ground beneath Knight. Pap was but four feet away. Pulling himself on to the boardwalk he slid around toward Pap.

'I lost my gun,' Knight cursed.

'Got a Winchester back here.' Pap was slipping two

more shotgun shells into the breech. Knight jacked a round into the Winchester and fired into the darkness. Then he fired again, sweeping the rifle randomly back and forth, filling the night with lead. Grunts of surprise and pain filled the air.

Eventually the tumult receded like a wave pulling back from a cantankerous shore and silence descended upon the town with a deathly finality. Then, far off, Pap and Knight could hear hoof beats in the distance.

Cautiously, Knight slipped close to the jail door and with a sweep of his arm sent the chairs blocking the way crashing aside. He kicked open the door then, throwing caution aside as well, for he needed only to confirm what he already knew.

The door to the jail room was slightly ajar and remarkably, defying the blast that had torn out part of the wall, an oil lamp still sat on the sheriff's desk, painting the room with a yellow cast. The cell, of course, was empty. Just enough of the adobe wall had been blown apart. A small enough hole had been the result of a carefully placed stick of dynamite and by sheer force the two prisoners, aided by the cowpunchers, had been able to slip through the rubble.

Once again Knight cursed under his breath.

Far out over the mountains the black sky writhed like a giant beast and he saw lightning flash like serpents' tongues in a boiling mass of clouds. A cold, mocking breeze swept across the town and vanished into the desert.

'I reckon they got what they wanted.' Pap's voice was thick with tension.

'They got 'em all right.' Knight's mouth was dry. His temples throbbed. 'But they paid a price. Come morning the undertaker's hammer will be kept busy pounding nails into new coffins.'

'I reckon it's over then,' Pap said.

'How do you figure?'

Pap looked up in surprise. 'You can't be figuring we'll go after them now. Them boys got murder in their souls. We ain't got a chance.'

'I don't see it that way at all.'

Pap rubbed a hand stained with gunpowder across his bearded jaw. Knight went into the jail again and returned carrying the lantern. The flame flickered alive as he turned up the wick. With the lamp in his hand he searched the street for his gun, ignoring the lifeless stares of the dead men whose pale faces caught the lamp's glare as he swept the lantern back and forth. When he found his gun he holstered it and joined Pap on the boardwalk.

Pap studied the aging marshal a moment. Finally he said, 'You and Tibbs are cut from the same cloth. Maybe ya'll be kin to Lazarus. Well, dagnabit, if you're gonna play this out I reckon I'm foolish enough to finish it with you.'

Knight nodded but said nothing. He squinted into the darkness. Somewhere out amongst that unending stretch of darkness Les and Edgar Usher were roaming free, but Knight understood something they hadn't realized yet. They had nowhere to go. Nowhere at all.

CHAPTER FIFTEEN

Cole Tibbs stepped into his former home with his gun drawn. The house was deathly silent, the air thick with the stench of being closed in for too long. The main hall was lit by candelabras and oil lamps. In the yellow glow the dark furniture and heavy drapery cast a grim pall over the scene. He brushed aside memories of his childhood when this house was open to the sunlight, the sounds of merriment and contentment ringing off the walls.

Usher had changed all of that. In the end his father had been swindled by a man far more ruthless than anyone had anticipated, and it cost him his life. Tibbs had wrestled with his agony a long time, had come to recognize it for what it was, and long ago accepted that sentiment would not bring Usher to justice. And maybe the law wouldn't either. Usher was playing a far deadlier game.

He strode quietly down the hall and stepped into the den where he'd faced Usher just two days before. The room was empty. Tibbs wasn't surprised. Knight had told him something of his war experiences, and the hatred that simmered beneath the charming southern personalities that refused to accept their fate. Democracy would always be in danger from isolationists and the hell-spawned raiders who planted the seeds of discontent. Usher would fight to the death.

He stood motionless in the room and listened. The wind had died down and the house was silent but for the occasional creaking floorboard. Tibbs visualized the house in his mind. Up the stairs and down another hall. That was where the floorboard had creaked. Usher had taken Jamie upstairs. It was a good defensive position. Tibbs wouldn't be able to ascend the stairs and avoid Usher's fire. He would be cut down on the stairs.

Grimly, he went from the room and slipped outside. Alongside the mansion's eastside there stood a utility shed where the Mexicans had kept tools and miscellaneous equipment for the livery. He holstered his gun. Tibbs climbed on to a barrel and heaved himself on to the shed's creaking roof. From here he managed to pull himself up on to a second story balcony. He knew the heavy glass and oak framed doors were unlocked. As a boy he had slipped out of the house in this manner often enough.

He went inside. This had been his room. He was startled to find the room empty. There was no furniture, not even a chair. Unadorned whitewashed walls stared back at him. The scent of dust and mildew hung in the air. He doubted then if anyone had entered this room in years.

Pulling his gun, he crept to the door and cracked it open. With his eyes adjusting to the gloom he could discern a yellow aura from the lamps. The hall and stairwell were flung with shadows. He slipped into the hall and began making his way toward the west wing. He turned a corner and paused. This stretch of hallway was dark. There were two doors on his left and straight ahead stood an oak door that opened up into a large room. He believed Usher held Jamie captive in that room.

He stood transfixed by the darkness, listening, assessing his options. There was no other entrance into the room. In this section of hallway the oil lamps had been snuffed and the scent of smoke lingered in the air.

Usher was waiting for him.

Tibbs needed a solution. Charging the door with his gun blazing might get Jamie killed. But Usher was undoubtedly alone. If Tibbs could determine Usher's location he might chance a shot through the wall as he charged.

No good. Usher had himself boxed in but Tibbs couldn't approach without serious injury to himself. There had to be another way.

He backed up, slowly, reversing his path until he was once again around the corner. He holstered his gun. He thought about the room. There was one window and he might be able to. . . .

Quickly, having decided on a course of action, he went back to his room and entered the balcony. He looked up hoping to find a handhold but the roof was three feet out of reach. Then he remembered the attic. He returned to the hall and entered a small room on the east end. From here he pulled down the ladder and ascended into the attic. Brushing past an old trunk and several broken chairs, he stooped before the attic window. The bronze latch was rusty and stiff beneath his fingers. He gave it a twist and the attic window pushed outward on a squealing hinge.

He stopped. There was nothing he could do. If Usher had heard the sound – and he probably had – he wouldn't necessarily fathom what Tibbs was doing. He had to chance it. Angling himself through the window he twisted his body and gripped the roof. Swinging his right leg up as his left foot braced against the window, he heaved himself on to the roof.

The distant rumble of thunder caught his attention and looking westward he saw another mass of clouds stretching across the desert sky. He made his way across the peaked roof, and presently he heard gunfire. Soon he paused again as a sudden blast shattered the stillness. The sound had emanated from Raven Flats but a glance in that direction revealed only the dark silhouettes of buildings and perhaps faintly a light burning in a solitary window. A rush of rifle fire echoed across the dark desert and Tibbs knew instinctively that Knight wasn't finished.

He continued across the roof as the rifle fire ceased. Eventually he reached the precipice and stood directly above the only window into the room where he believed Jamie was held captive.

He crouched, examined the window, turned his body and slipped over the edge. His boots barely had surface to balance him as he eased himself down still holding the ledge. From this position he could kick in the window and fling himself into the room. He had no other plan than that, trusting now in providence to align the circumstances to his benefit.

His right knee cocked and he kicked in the window with a crash and before a second had passed he slammed his body through the splintered glass and shattered lattice, his body smashing on to the floor.

He was up in an instant, his hand dropping for his Colt, when Usher's tactical brilliance became evident. A large man roared from the darkness, the hammer of his Colt clicking back, and Tibbs charged, knocking the gun from the man's hand, his own Colt still hanging uselessly in his holster.

A fist cracked into his jaw and Tibbs saw stars explode behind his eyelids. His own fist lashed out, hard, once, twice, each time slamming into bone. The big man grunted and faltered. Tibbs again reached for his gun but the man bulled into him head first. They went down in a tangle of flailing fists. Tibbs kicked out with his leg, catching the man on the knee. Something splintered and the man yowled in pain.

Rolling swiftly, Tibbs leaped to his feet as the man stumbled his way, another fist slamming into him. They circled, warily. In the dim glow Tibbs could just make out the man's features. He was a big brute with a sloped brow like a monkey, small dark eyes, and all too powerful arms. He was breathing through his nose, his cheeks puffing from exertion.

'I ain't got a gun now,' the man said, flashing a toothless grin. 'A lawman won't kill an unarmed man.'

Then the man spit into his palms and rubbed his hands together. 'C'mon,' he said. 'C'mon, lawman!' The big brute's face was carved into a sinister sneer.

Tibbs should have shot the man then. Max Knight probably would have shot him and gone from the room. But Tibbs couldn't shoot him.

Tibbs eyed his opponent and assessed the odds. The man was bigger and stronger, but he had already hurt him badly. And he couldn't afford a prolonged fight. He had to find Usher and Jamie. But now there was no choice.

He jabbed his left fist into the man's mouth, snapping

his head back. Following with a right, his balled fist cracked against the man's face just below his left eye. Tibbs felt the skin tear loose from his knuckles as his fist connected with bone. The man was staggered but he caught Tibbs in the chest with a hammer-like fist. Tibbs stepped back, his chest feeling as if it might collapse from the strike. The brute was incredibly strong.

Wheeling about each other, boots scuffling along the floorboards, the two men proceeded to pummel each other mercilessly. Tibbs worked at the man's ribs, continuously sending blistering jabs and punches and hoping to slow him down. The man was limping from the kick to his knee and after a flurry of stinging punches Tibbs kicked at the knee again. The brute screamed, nearly toppled, but fixed his gaze on Tibbs with a look of unrelenting hatred.

'C'mon, boy. I promise to kill ya quick. I'll snap yer neck and ya can join the angels.'

Spittle and blood flung from the man's busted lips as he talked. His voice was hollow, devoid of intelligence, but simmering with the atavistic fury of an ape.

Tibbs concentrated on the man. His right leg was useless. But Tibbs had to avoid getting clenched by those powerful arms.

Just shoot him!

The desire to finish the man with a bullet was overpowering, but Tibbs fought against the urge. He wouldn't resort to the less than honorable tactics of killers like Usher and his men, and although nobody would ever know if Tibbs decided to shoot the brute down, he knew he couldn't live with himself. He had seen enough of violence, and of violent men, to know there had to be a better way.

126

He lashed out with his fist, caught the man in the eye, kicked him again, but in the other knee. His boot heel cracked bone. Howling, the man unleashed a torrent of punches that slammed into Tibbs with a tornado's velocity. He reeled backward, nearly losing his balance. Then the brute was at his throat. Clammy, powerful hands gripped his neck and squeezed. The man's thumbs dug into his larynx. Tibbs could smell the brute's sour breath laced with whiskey, his pungent body odor that of a caged animal. Gagging, losing his breath, pain lancing his throat, Tibbs began to methodically slam punches into the man's face.

Life was reduced to the sound of knuckles beating against flesh, the splintering sound of the brute's nose breaking, and the air salted by the tang of blood. Tibbs swung the man about, forcing pressure on his knees. He had little time. He swung again and they were out the door. Slowly he walked the man backward toward the stairwell at the corner.

His fist was soaked with the man's blood but still the brute would not relent. What hell-spawn creature had Usher set against him? Some dull drifter with no past and no future, a whore's forgotten offspring finally lured by an offer of riches untold. Angered by these thoughts, Tibbs kicked again at the injured knee, and then again. It was difficult going in such close quarters, but then, after another vicious kick, the brute released his hands.

Screaming in pain, the man sank to his knees and Tibbs kicked again while he was off-balance. His large body slammed against the rail, the wood splintering under the brute's weight. Without hesitation Tibbs kicked again, this time at the man's chest. The rail gave way and the brute dropped like a boulder into the darkened foyer, his body crashing on to the floorboards with a sickening crunch.

Tibbs leaned against the wall staring at the darkness beyond the broken rail. His breath was coming in wheezing gasps and sweat stung his eyes.

How many other brutes did Usher have hidden in this house of horrors? And where was Jamie?

Tibbs sucked in a lungful of air and pulled his gun. A fury overtook him, consumed him. He kicked open doors. He overturned tables. He crashed through closets. In each room he entered he found – nothing. The house had been gutted long ago and had become but a shell to keep out the rain. Not even his memories belonged here any longer.

He went downstairs. The brute's body lay in a jumble of broken limbs, a dark pool splashed next to his twisted head like a glimmering shadow.

He searched every room. When he found Pete Usher he felt a momentary sting of pity. Pete lay on his cot in a sparsely furnished room. His breathing was labored. The bandage on his leg was stained a dark red and his leg had swollen to the point where it appeared it might burst. Pete held a gun in his hand. He was sweating. His eyes cradled a feeble spark of life in the hollow sockets.

'Pa wants to ride soon,' he said. 'He's got a notion to ride against that US marshal you've taken up with.'

The voice was nearly a whisper, but unfaltering. Tibbs came up along the cot.

'Where's the old man?'

Pete chuckled, a faint and eerie cackle. 'He's here. You'll find him soon enough. I got a fever now. Lost too much blood. Damn you for coming back.'

'Is the girl with him?'

'I never saw no girl.'

'Jamie Hart. Your pa has her as a prisoner.'

That eerie cackle again. Something that might have been a grin stretched across Pete Usher's face like a shadow.

'She's a pretty one. She always had a shine for you. I hope he kills her.'

Pete began coughing. It was terrible to watch but Tibbs stood unmoving next to the cot. His face was pale, the hollow eyes squinting in pain, his chest heaving as he hacked and coughed. When the coughing subsided his body visibly relaxed. His eyes flicked open and close and then focused on Tibbs.

'Pa gave me this gun. Said to use it if I wasn't man enough to ride against you and that marshal.'

'I can get you a doctor when this is over.'

'It's over. It'll be the undertaker that makes a profit tomorrow.'

Tibbs walked to the door. He looked back at Pete Usher once, then turned his back on him and strode down the hall. A moment later the gunshot shattered the stillness.

Aimlessly he wandered into the den. This room, above all others had the most furniture. An oil lamp still burned on the desk. Candles in brass holders flickered on an oak hutch. He stepped around the desk, turned, and examined the room from another angle. There was a large trunk with brass latches pressed up against the wall. Its round top and ancient wood bespoke of travels long past. A seaman's trunk. He didn't remember seeing it when he'd faced Usher in this room. He stepped forward, then stopped.

129

Some inner sense warned him and he slowly turned his head to the left.

The long damask draperies, black against dark walls, seemed to rustle and there he saw two fierce glows like red flames in a brazier. Usher's feral eyes reflected the candle flames and the old man stepped out of the shadows, the Navy Colt extended in his hand.

'Yes, she's in the trunk. I daresay she may have suffocated by now.' Usher pulled back the gun's hammer and fired, but the hammer stuck hollowly against the percussion cap. A misfire!

Before Tibbs could fire Usher had leapt forth, slashing his gun at Tibbs and tearing a gash on his chin. And again Usher slashed at him, eyes blazing with an unholy gleam, his thin lips pulled back in a snarl. Tibbs dropped his Colt, fell, and covered his head with his hands.

Usher fled. Tibbs saw the dovetailed coat fly past him as the old man raced out the door. He scrambled across the floor, grabbed his gun and quickly smashed the trunk's lock with his gun's grip. He flung open the trunk. Jamie was huddled with her hands tied behind her back. He pulled her gently up. Her skin was pale, her eyes closed and for an instant he thought she was gone.

But then he realized that she was breathing and her eyelids fluttered open. Lifting her from the trunk he swiftly untied her hands.

'Jamie!'

Her cheeks were blushed, tears began streaming down her face.

'Cole!' she gasped, then she shoved him away, anger flooding her face. 'You should have told me you were a lawman!'

'There's no time for this. I have to stop Usher.' Tibbs grabbed her by the arm. 'Let's go! I want you safe before I go after him.'

Pulling her into the hall, Tibbs was about to take Jamie out to Conchita when Usher fired from the stairwell. The bark of the Navy Colt echoed loudly and the lead ball grazed Tibbs on the arm before thumping into the wall. He pushed Jamie out the door.

'Find Conchita at the bunkhouse!' he commanded. 'Stay with her until I come for you!'

Jamie went without speaking, but Tibbs had seen the anger, fear and confusion on her face. They would have a lot to talk about once this was over.

He followed Usher up the stairs, bounding up the steps two at a time. He caught up with him on the landing. The old man turned and fired again – and again the Colt misfired! But Tibbs was surprised by Usher's dexterity. Flinging himself at Tibbs, the old man once again used his gun as a club. With his left fist, Tibbs struck Usher in the jaw. The old man was staggered, but he swung at Tibbs, blindly, furiously, an animal-like sound screeching from between his lips.

Usher managed to pull the hammer back and fire his gun. The gun popped, flame at the muzzle, and a lead ball seared across Tibbs' arm. Grunting, Tibbs faltered, and Usher used the opportunity to disappear into the darkened hall.

'You damn fool!' Tibbs spat. 'Where do you hope to go? This is finished. Give it up!'

Silence greeted Tibbs as he peered into the hallway.

Tibbs was restless, and tired. He didn't want to waste time searching each room again. The old man was only prolonging the inevitable. He had one shot in that old Navy Colt and it might even be another misfire. He wondered if Usher had another gun. He doubted it. That old Navy Colt had been with Usher since the war. The old killer was sentimental and now time had worked against him as those percussion caps began to cause misfires.

A sound caught his attention. It came from the room closest to him. Tibbs entered the room and there stood Usher, his thin frame and pale features illuminated by the oil lamp he'd just lit. Usher held the lamp aloft in his left hand, in his right hand the Navy Colt with its last shot was pointing at Tibbs.

'Drop your gun.'

Tibbs appraised Usher. His breath came out in a raspy, wheezing whine that reminded Tibbs of a dying man's death rattle, and maybe it was.

'You've had two misfires in that old gun.'

'The odds are still high that the last shot will still find its mark.'

'You have a weakness for old things. One of us will gamble successfully now.'

Tibbs had his Colt aimed at Usher's chest. They faced each other in a stalemate. The oil lamp cast weird shadows across Usher's face. At this distance, and under the flickering glow of the oil lamp, Usher looked like a corpse long in the grave. Such was the countenance of decay on his features that Tibbs shivered with disgust when those blazing eyes stared back at him with condemnation.

'Your father was a fool, too. I'm pleased that I ordered his death.' Usher's tone was mocking.

'You've lost two sons. One by his own hand. Maxfield Knight will be handling Les and Edgar. What are you

132

hoping to accomplish here?'

'Your death!' Usher said with finality, and he pulled the trigger.

The gun misfired for a final time and with a shriek Usher sprang at Tibbs.

Tibbs fired, his bullet blasting through Usher's belly, but the old man never wavered. He swung the oil lamp at Tibbs but he side-stepped and the lamp shattered against the damask drapery, setting it on fire. The flames crept up the drapery, cackling like a demon.

Usher clung to Tibbs, his bony hands grasping his throat. Usher was light, almost skeletal, and Tibbs brought the gun up and fired through his chest. The blast flung Usher against the drapes, his long white hair igniting and for a second his body twitched as his hair burned. Tibbs emptied his Colt into the writhing body, finishing the old man at last, and then, horrified, his stepped back as the flames roared to life. In seconds the fire had grown into a conflagration. The old timbers would burn quickly.

With a sudden shudder Usher's burning body was obliterated by flames, the arms suddenly jerking spasmodically. Sickened, Tibbs turned away.

His own face reddened by the flames, Tibbs stepped back, shielding his face with his arm as the fire whooshed across the drapes, clinging to the walls. He stumbled out into the hallway. Already the smoke was thick, clogging the air, flooding the hall like angry spirits.

He went down the stairs, the flames crackling behind him. Jamie, Conchita, and the old Mexican were standing near the porch when he emerged from the house. Jamie approached him quickly.

'Is he. . . ?'

'Yes, he's dead.' Tibbs looked up at the house. Flames were wavering in the windows, creeping along the outer walls.

'It's over then.' Jamie said.

'No it's not.' Tibbs said quickly. He looked into Jamie's expectant face, and at Conchita and the old man. 'We have to get out of here until we make certain Les and Edgar are behind bars. And Hagard is still out there somewhere.'

'Cole! This is madness. Where can we possibly go?' Jamie's voice was thick with tension. Tibbs looked into her soft eyes and forced a smile. Then he turned his gaze out to the dark expanse of desert where the Usher boys had killed his father all of those years ago.

'Snakebite Creek,' he said quietly.

CHAPTER SIXTEEN

After a thunderstorm the desert is a landscape in transition. All signs of the rain that had fallen in torrents were erased by the whispering sands. But the rain's effect was not lost on the myriad wildlife and plants that thrived in a place desolate to man but not unknown to the Apache. The chuparosa shrubbery that thrived along the rocky slopes near Snakebite Creek were home to insects, jack rabbits, and the tarantula. At a glance a man would not see the telltale drift of a tarantula crawling from beneath the sparse shade; nor would he notice the trilling hum of insects in the underbrush, but Cole Tibbs recognized the sound and before lifting the canvas that had protected Jamie and him all through the night he knew that once again the desert had awakened.

Jamie blinked against the blistering sunlight as she slipped from beneath the canvas. Late the previous night, fearing that Hagard and his men would find them, Cole had brought her here and together they had huddled under the canvas as the storm played out over the desert. The depression between the rocks that Cole had wanted to hide in, however, had been flooded by the rain and so they had been forced to seek higher ground where Cole had held her trembling in his arms until she had fallen asleep. The hot sun on the canvas had awakened them.

For Jamie it was as if the darkness had fled with Usher's spirit for the world appeared then bright and promising. She marveled at the cream-colored ghost flowers and desert willows that ranged in clusters about the landscape. A bird circled in the sky, perhaps a raven, the only ominous sign in an otherwise pastoral scene.

With the rain pounding against the canvas all night, and with the fearsome sight of Carleton Usher still fresh in her mind, she had found comfort in Cole's arms, grateful that he was a gentleman, but worried about what the morning would bring. The desert's beauty dispelled all of her fears, which was a fatal error so many unwary travelers had made on their trek throughout the southwest.

Tibbs stood beside Jamie, looking at her, and ignoring the landscape.

'I owe you an apology,' he began.

She turned and faced him and her beauty suddenly had him spellbound. Her dark hair caught the morning light, and her graceful, supple figure stood out in contrast to the ragged rocks and crucifixion shrubs that gave the area its harsh tone.

'Why didn't you tell me you were a deputy US marshal?'

'I thought you'd be better off the less you knew. But things happened quickly. . . .'

'You mean the killing began quickly?' Her tone was hard, unsympathetic.

'These men are born killers. They haven't given Knight and I much choice.'

'And this man, Maxfield Knight, what I've heard about

him disturbs me.'

'He's a difficult man to understand, but he's an honest lawman.'

'Cole, when will the killing end?' She looked away, her expression hard.

He lifted her chin with his hand and looked deeply into her eyes. A lot of time had passed but Tibbs had always had a fondness for this girl. He tried to think of something to say but began to feel uncomfortable as she gazed back at him.

Then a shout rang out and the moment was broken. One of Hagard's men, circling the area, had spotted them from a distance. Tibbs cursed. He should have checked the area first.

'Down here.'

They slid into the depression that had been flooded only hours before. The rainwater had already evaporated under the hot morning sun or had trickled away. Tibbs pulled his gun and punched out the empty shells from his showdown with Carleton Usher. He replaced the cartridges and slipped the gun into his holster. He wished he'd brought a Winchester. Their only hope was to get their hands on a horse and ride hard for Raven Flats. They would never make it across the desert trail on foot now that they'd been seen. This hiding place was only good if it remained a secret.

'Follow me.'

Jamie followed him as he crouched low and slid around the rocks. They had enough cover in the rocks but the area was too small for a prolonged gunfight. Then again, Tibbs decided, Max Knight's appearance might be enough to turn the tide. The sooner Knight arrived – and

Tibbs had unwavering faith in the man's ability to survive – the sooner they could finish this fight.

He peered over the rocks.

A solitary rider was making his way carefully across the creek. He would pass within twenty feet of their former hiding place. Tibbs waited until the man was closer, then he stood up. Startled, the man went for his gun, but before he could fire Tibbs had crouched low again, pulling Jamie after him.

'Where are we going?' Jamie asked breathlessly.

'We have to keep them guessing awhile. Then the lead's gonna start flying. When that happens you stay down until it's over.'

They made their way back to the depression between the rocks and Tibbs peered over the other side. Six riders were whipping leather to get their horses into position. In another few minutes they would have Tibbs and Jamie surrounded.

This is as good a time as any, thought Tibbs.

He stood up, gun in hand, and fired quickly at the closest rider. Most men couldn't make a shot like that with a revolver, but Tibbs had spent seven years practicing with his Colt. He could hit a large target at a hundred yards, as could any capable gunman. Most men simply weren't capable gunmen.

His bullet struck the man in the shoulder. He howled, dropping his gun. Tibbs fired again, but this time on a rider just behind the wounded man. It was a longer shot, albeit only by a few feet, but once again his bullet found its mark. The rider flipped backward from his saddle, a bloom of red on his shirt.

Tibbs squinted against the sun. Shouts were rising in

the distance followed by galloping hoofbeats. Men were shouting and whooping as a bullet shattered against the rocks, a spray of disintegrating lead and rock chips stinging their faces like needles. He slid down into a crevice and quickly crawled ten feet before sticking his head over the rim.

Les and Edgar Usher were nearby on horseback. Feliciano was with them. He didn't see Hagard. He was being flanked. What would Knight do? And where was Knight anyway?

Tibbs decided to hold his fire. He wanted each shot to count. He couldn't waste bullets on diversionary tactics. Not this time.

Then he heard boots crunching on the rocks. Two men on foot had been sent to flush him out. They came over the rocks quickly, spaced about twenty feet apart. They hadn't seen him yet. Tibbs fired immediately, his thumb at the hammer, the Colt roaring and as the first man fell he shot the second man in the chest. The sound of his thundering Colt echoed across the rocks. The men had fallen silently, dead before they sprawled across the boulder.

A raven swept across the sky, cawing, and its shrill lament sent a chill down his spine.

'Give it up, Tibbs! We'll kill the girl the minute we see her.' Les Usher's voice boomed across the rocks. 'You don't have a chance. Surrender now and we'll let the girl live!'

Fury hammered through Tibbs. He stood up, almost too calmly, and the sight of him standing there unnerved the men on horseback.

'What the hell's he doing?' a voice said.

'Shoot him!' another voice said.

Tibbs willed himself to remain calm, his eyes taking in every movement, every man's position. Before they could draw their own guns his Colt blazed. A man toppled from his horse, his gun discharging harmlessly into the sand. Les and Edgar, who had wisely positioned themselves behind a group of four men, reined their mounts and retreated.

Tibbs slipped away through the rocks and glanced at Jamie. She was still hunched down in the crevice between the boulders. Her eyes found his, questioningly, and he gave her a thumbs up signal. It was all he could think to do. He knew he had to appear confident or she would panic.

When her eyes widened in fear he wheeled about in time to stop another man on foot. Tibbs fired, his bullet striking the man in the arm. He dropped his gun and charged. He was too close and too fast for Tibbs to fire again. The man had swiftly pulled a Bowie knife. Tibbs chopped at the man's wrist but he held tightly on to the knife. Tibbs struck with his boot at the man's groin. He grunted but remained standing. The man launched a fist at Tibbs that sent him sprawling backward, his Colt flung from his hands. Then with a roar the man was on Tibbs.

They rolled across the rocks, Tibbs holding the man's arm to prevent the Bowie knife from slicing him open. The man's fetid breath made Tibbs recoil in disgust. Tibbs headbutted the man, shattering his nose, but still he held on. They were locked in a deadly embrace, blood streaming from the man's broken nose, Tibbs holding both his arms.

A voice nearby yelled, 'Barstow has him!' There was movement behind him, then a Colt blazing. The gunshot

140

echoed like mocking laughter across the rocks. Barstow grunted, the bullet having torn a hole in his chest. His eyes remained fixed on Tibbs as the life slowly ebbed from his body. Tibbs finally pushed the man aside, the knife clattering against the boulder. He turned to see Jamie holding his Colt. She had stood frozen in place after shooting Barstow.

'I'll take the gun.' Tibbs said. He took the gun from her and noticed that her hand was trembling, but only a little. 'You have a lot of brass. You saved my life. Now get down.'

Before she could protest Tibbs was up on the rocks again and he quickly fired at the advancing men. There were more curses as Usher's men retreated again.

'He got Barstow!' a voice said.

Tibbs ducked low, and hunched down next to Jamie. She had gotten Barstow all right, and he had gotten a few others, but there were plenty of men left to fight. Tibbs looked at his saddle-bag. He had enough ammunition to hold them off for a long while, but eventually they would breech his defensive position by force of numbers.

He punched out the empty brass and reloaded his Colt. They would need reinforcements, and quickly.

'What are we going to do?' Jamie asked.

'Don't worry,' Tibbs said reassuringly, 'Max Knight is out there somewhere.'

'But he's only one man.'

'Trust me. Max Knight is a lot more dangerous than any of these men.'

'You better be right,' Jamie said, 'or we're in trouble.'

CHAPTER SEVENTEEN

Maxfield Knight and Pap Wingfoot were hunkered down in a strand of scrub brush two hundred yards from Snakebite Creek when the shooting began.

'Well that does it,' Pap said. 'They started without us.'

'Downright rude of them,' Knight said.

They began walking toward the creek, eyes on the landscape.

'How do you figure this will play out?' Pap asked.

'We go in shooting.'

'You won't give them a chance to surrender?'

'Usher didn't surrender when General Lee surrendered in '65. There's no reason for him to surrender now. He has us outgunned and Tibbs is surrounded. His sons are free so the way he sees it he can just kill us all.'

'We sure can't let that happen,' Pap said, spitting a stream of tobacco juice into the sand.

'No we can't.'

'So you think old man Usher is still alive after facing Tibbs or maybe we're just up against his sons?'

'It doesn't matter. If Tibbs killed the old man his sons

will face a reckoning.'

'You rode with General Sherman to the sea?'

'I did.'

'Heard stories about you. Never believed much of it until now.'

Knight grunted.

They were a hundred yards out and saw the riders skirting the swell of rocks.

'We're gonna have to be careful of the rattlesnakes,' Pap said. 'A man dies right quick from a rattler's bite.'

'Lead poisoning is faster,' Knight said. Pap glanced at Knight but didn't respond.

They could see a good stretch of the landscape that rose and dipped around Snakebite Creek. The sun was hot and relentless on their backs as they picked their way amongst the cactus and spindly brush. Five men on horseback held themselves back from the core group of riders that flanked the rocky swell where they knew Tibbs was holed up, undoubtedly with Jamie Hart.

'I'll come at them from the southwest,' Knight said. 'You come through that creek. Get up into that grassy area and call out to Tibbs.'

'That's where the snakes are,' Pap said glumly.

'Use that scattergun.'

'That's bound to stir up everything all right,' Pap said. 'Snakes and two-legged gunmen too. It's gonna be a long afternoon.'

Pap moved off, cursing under his breath.

Knight wended his way through the sun-scorched landscape, doing his best to keep out of sight. The echo of gunfire had diminished and the riders were reconnoitering with the two Usher brothers. They would powwow and decide on another course of action. But Knight could see their options were limited. From his concealed position Tibbs could hold them off a long while. Their only hope would be to rush him. But the Usher boys weren't ready for that yet.

Three small birds suddenly took flight from their perch in a spindly bush and a man on horseback galloped hard toward the marshal. Knight shot the man, blowing him from the saddle. He tumbled backwards off the horse. He saw the riders in the distance look his way. *Time to take the offensive*, Knight thought.

He chased the horse, caught the bridle, and eased the horse to a halt before swinging into the saddle. The saddle boot held a Winchester. He pulled it up, jacked a round into the breech, and reined the horse toward the distant group. They split into three groups, the Usher brothers still holding back. The group on his left was closest to him. Knight spurred the horse into a gallop and rode at the men.

There was a moment of hesitation as the four riders stared at him incredulously, no doubt shocked that he wasn't riding away. Then they charged, Colts coming up into their hands. None of the men had thought to use a rifle.

Knight shot the furthest man with a single fluid motion, jacked free the brass which spun off into the air like a gold tooth, and then his horse closed the distance. It was, at that moment for Knight, like something he had read in a book called *Ivanhoe* where the hero engages in a jousting match. Except Knight was using a Winchester instead of a lance.

A bullet grazed his arm and he fired again, blowing

144

another man screaming from his saddle. Then he swept past the two remaining men so quickly they had no time to stop. He reined his horse, wheeling about, and spurred the animal again. His Winchester blew flame from the muzzle and a third man bellowed in pain, clutching his side. The last rider looked at Knight, fear plainly etched on his face, and spurred his horse away. Knight let him go. The man was heading for the desert. Knight knew the man would ride on, find a border town and get drunk. Deserters always followed a pattern.

Les and Edgar Usher dismounted and scattered. In the blink of an eye they had disappeared into the rolling wash of sand, mesquite, and cactus. Then the other riders dismounted to be swallowed by the vast and deceptive desert. So far all of them were north of Tibbs. Pap was on the south end, somewhere in the tall grassy area.

When Knight thought the sun couldn't get hotter, the air suddenly seemed warmer. Whatever cool breezes had blown in with the previous night's storm were forgotten. Now only the sun held dominion over all; only the sun mattered as the world settled into a stifling furnace of suffocating heat. The dry, hot sand remained motionless in the still morning light. Nothing stirred. Then faintly, and nearly imperceptibly, he heard a distant rattle. Pap would have to be very careful. In this heat the rattlesnakes would slither on to the heat blasted rocks to warm their cold blooded souls. If they had souls.

Knight went for the rocks. He would have to cross a hundred dangerous yards where any one of Usher's men might now be hiding.

A shotgun boomed.

One of Usher's men had just found Pap Wingfoot.

Knight went toward the sound.

Meticulously and purposefully, Knight cut a path across the sand, shielded by the swell of earth and profusion of scrub, until he circled the rocks where Tibbs was hiding. He thought about calling out to Tibbs but changed his mind. He was sweating. Those horses had canteens looped on to their saddle horns and if he could get close enough he planned on taking one. But the water would only matter if this gun battle lasted too long, he thought.

Muffled voices caught his attention.

The voices were on his left, and he turned as two men scrambled for cover.

A stick of dynamite whistled through the air, and then he was galloping. The dynamite stick arced through the air, a thin gray line of smoke trailing from the fuse. He was flung from his panicked horse as the stick exploded. His horse had galloped in a haphazard direction and was soon lost from sight. There was a brief burst of sand clouding the air. He was up then, running again, hauling himself across the sand as a man emerged from behind a spindly bush and tossed another stick of dynamite in his direction. Knight fired and a blossom of red shattered across the man's chest, toppling him backward. The dynamite exploded thirty feet away, a shower of sand stinging his face.

Then another man was on Knight almost before he knew it. He squeezed the trigger in the same instant his peripheral vision picked up a shape leaping in his direction. The gun barked and jolted in his hand. The man fell into him, a fist cracking his jaw. Whipping his Colt across the man's face, Knight knocked him to the ground, leveled his gun, and blew the man into eternity.

146

He raced for the creek expecting another attack with dynamite but nothing happened. Without a second thought he went into the underbrush after Pap. He went downhill. There was no sound but for the telltale rattle in the grass and the unholy caw-caw of the blackbirds.

Pap suddenly stood up before him.

'I damn near shot you!' Pap said.

'You seen Tibbs?'

'He's hunkered down in those rocks with Jamie. It's a good spot. He can hold them until Christmas if he has enough cartridges.'

'Let's not make him wait that long.'

Pap glanced around warily. 'Those damn fools stirred up the rattlers with that dynamite.'

Knight saw the golden swirl of a diamondback disappear into the grass. The sound of agitated rattlers was ominously loud. His skin crawled.

'Let's go.'

Pap followed him across the grass and on to a rocky slope. He was about to call out to Tibbs when a spur jangled and Hagard and Feliciano appeared forty feet away. Hagard fired. His bullet chipped a rock near Knight's foot. They dodged for cover. Knight's reaction was instantaneous. His Colt was in his hand, spitting lead. He emptied the gun, flipped open the loading gate and ejected the brass. In one fluid movement he reloaded, thumbing six cartridges into the chamber. Hagard and Feliciano had taken cover.

'He's got that Mexican with him,' Pap said.

Knight was silent. Hagard and the Mexican were situated at the crux of a sloping trail. They were separated by boulders on each side which framed the trail like two obese statues. Tibbs and Jamie were just beyond, nestled in a shallow depression between the rocks.

Hagard had attacked in a rush and just as quickly disappeared. The bastard is testing us, Knight thought. His pulse throbbed, his temples flaring with pressure. Squinting against the sun he waited for any sign of movement. Knight looked around. They were in a small clearing against a sheer cliff wall. A trail on his far right led up into the rocks.

'Pap, you go up that way,' he said, pointing. 'Circle around to the other side and see if you can draw a bead on them, but leave the Mexican alone.'

Pap nodded. 'Feliciano's gotta problem, though. He's gotta make like he's with Hagard.'

'He'll think of something, but he won't fire on you.'

Pap went off and Knight continued to scrutinize the landscape.

A burst of movement shattered the stillness on his right. Then two of them came at once, running hard with guns aimed at Knight, and fast, like deer sprinting across the grasslands, determined to collect their bounty. The guns blazed and Knight was firing as Tibbs came over a boulder and fired on the two men. A gun barked and a man tumbled, wincing in pain. The gun barked again and the second man was dead. Knight nodded at Tibbs but had no time for talk. The killing time was upon them now and all he knew, as Usher had learned long ago, was the cold-hearted fury of battle.

With his gun roaring, a man was on him, yelling wildly, leaping forward, the pale gleam of a knife in his hand, sweeping a deadly path through the air. The man slammed into Knight, knocking the gun from his hand.

148

They went tumbling in a ball of dust. Knight grabbed for the man and spun him around. With a hard thrust he brought his knee up and he heard the crack as the man's ribs broke. The man screamed as his knife fell from his numb hand. Knight fell on the knife, scooping it up with a fistful of sand, and spinning, drove the blade into the man's ribs. A whoosh of stale air burst free as the blade sliced through a lung. Blood spread over Knight's hands. The man slumped to the ground and he pushed the body away.

He took a breath and tried to hold it a minute, but his pulse was pounding like a war drum in his temples, his breath coming in rasping gasps. It took him a moment to control his breathing. Then he scooped sand into his bloody palms and rubbed the blood from his hands. He found his gun, ejected the brass, and reloaded.

He heard the *click* of a hammer being pulled back.

'Drop it and turn around.' It was Hagard, his voice a sneer of evil triumph.

Knight held on to the gun, and turned his waist without moving his legs. Hagard and Feliciano stood twenty feet away. The dark barrel of Hagard's gun was pointed at Knight's belly.

'You don't drop it, I'll shoot you.'

'You're going to shoot me anyway,' Knight said. Another instant and he was prepared to lunge, firing at Hagard as he hit the ground.

But then Hagard pulled the trigger and the hammer clacked harmlessly on to an empty chamber. Knight knew the sound well – Hagard hadn't reloaded. Knight turned his body around as Hagard thumbed the hammer again, and again it clacked on to an empty cylinder.

149

'It's empty you damn fool,' Knight said.

Hagard, eyes widening in horror, screamed at Feliciano. 'Shoot him! Shoot him, you dumb Mexican! I'll pay you a thousand dollars in gold if you shoot him!'

Feliciano shrugged. He looked at Knight, then he slowly pulled his Colt from his holster, leveled it, swung it around and shot Hagard in the chest. The blast threw Hagard backward. His body flung out with his arms wide, his eyes still open in astonishment, a curl of gunpowder lifting from the red hole that had torn through his chest. His body quivered once and then was still.

Feliciano holstered his gun. 'I am sorry, *señor*,' he said. 'My aim is not so good. I will make a confession to Father Spillane on Sunday. I will say Hail Mary twenty-five times and ask the Holy Father for forgiveness.'

Then Feliciano adjusted his sombrero, wiped the sweat from his face with a silk neckerchief and walked away. Knight watched him go, a thin smile creased across his lips. Then he holstered his gun and went to see about Tibbs.

CHAPTER EIGHTEEN

Tibbs had spotted Pap across the creek and had hunkered down in the grass. He went back and eased up to Jamie.

'Time is our enemy now,' he said quietly.

'What do you mean?'

'We'll all need water soon, including them.' He gestured toward the desert. 'I saw some canteens on their horses but it won't be enough. Those boys have been moving around a lot and whoever is left will be thirsty.'

Jamie nodded. 'Cole, I want you know how sorry I am, about all of this. I wish it had never happened to you.'

Tibbs nodded and scratched his jaw. 'It's all right, Jamie. Things will look a lot better once we finish this.' He squinted into the distance. 'I think the odds are still in our favor. There's a lot of bodies around now. Max has been busy.'

'And when the killing is over, what then?'

Tibbs looked at her and her eyes were deep emerald pools, pleading. He had to look away. She placed her hand on his arm.

'I don't know,' he said without looking at her. 'I have my duties with the US marshals service. My home base is

Colorado now, Knight is from Montana. Sometimes we have to travel. . . .' His voice trailed off. He didn't know what else to say. Jamie removed her hand from his arm. She was about to speak when Tibbs picked up a sound nearby.

'Cole!' It was Max Knight.

Knight came up over the rocks quickly followed by Pap.

'Nice little place you have here,' Pap said.

'How many do you think are left?' Tibbs asked.

'Maybe four including the Usher boys. The Mexican left after killing Hagard.'

'Feliciano killed Hagard?'

Knight nodded. 'Shot him dead right quick.'

Tibbs cast an eye on the desert surrounding them. 'Les and Edgar have split up. They must be circling around. I think it's time we took this fight to them.' Tibbs looked at Jamie, then at Pap. 'I need you to stay with her while we finish this.'

Pap spit a wad of chewing tobacco on to the rocks and rubbed his whiskers. 'I reckon I can do that if you two promise not to dally.'

'Not to what?'

'Dally. It means don't go moseying about like a bull looking for a heifer. Time's a'wasting and I got myself a powerful thirst. This heat won't go away anytime soon.'

Tibbs shook his head and chuckled. 'We'll be back soon enough.'

They followed the trail out of the rocks warily. After a while they stopped and listened but there was only the sound of wind moving over and between rocks, sometimes kicking up little dust funnels or whistling eerily between the cactus. It was a warm wind and it had come up suddenly, surprising them.

Knight was quiet and Tibbs thought he was absorbing the beauty of the sky and the enormous vista of desert around them, but after a minute it was apparent he was studying their location. The morning was fading and the afternoon's long shadows were already creeping from beneath the mesquite and cactus.

They kept close to the rocks, stepping carefully. They spotted numerous snakes either lazing on the rocks or slithering away as they approached. Tibbs was thirsty, his heart hammering in his ears. It had been a long night and he wanted to finish the deadly game that had been set in motion all of those years ago. Knight's gaze moved beyond the shimmering heat mirages and mottled scrub that skirted the area. His keen senses were ever alert for sound.

Knight scowled. Where had the Usher brothers gone?

They picked their way across the sand, making a wide circle around the rocks, crossing Snakebite Creek, gingerly moving through the tall grass, eventually returning to the northwest apex of their search. Buzzards circled in the sky and the scent of death was strong in the air.

Then they heard a scream – Jamie's shriek – which was quickly muffled.

Without speaking, Knight and Tibbs separated.

Tibbs took the shortest distance across the rocks while Knight circled around the long way.

A shout came from the rocks ahead of him.

'Come in Tibbs, and slowly! I have the woman. The old man is alive but I'll shoot him now if you don't answer!'

Grudgingly, Tibbs holstered his gun and stepped on to the boulder and looked down into the shallow depression that had been his hiding place just hours before. Les

153

Usher had a gun at Jamie's head. Pap was slumped to the side, a bloody gash on his forehead.

'Where's that marshal?' Usher asked. 'I'll kill her if you try anything!'

'I don't know,' Tibbs responded. He had to play for time. 'He was wounded and I left him back a ways. He might have crawled off and died for all I know.'

'Unbuckle that gunbelt.'

Tibbs unbuckled his gunbelt, trying to appear calm.

'Where's your brother?'

Maxfield Knight came over the boulder behind Les and walked slowly up behind him. Tibbs wanted to keep Les occupied.

'You and your brother have to face trial for embezzlement. You can surrender now.'

Les Usher was astounded. 'You loco bastard! I can shoot you right now!'

Knight was twenty feet away, then ten feet away. Tibbs had never seen a man move so quietly across rocks. Knight eased up behind Les with practiced stealth.

'You won't shoot me,' Tibbs said.

'What? Why the hell not?'

Knight raised his Colt and placed the barrel one inch from the back of his head and said to Les, 'Because I'll blow your brains out if you do.'

Knight thumbed back the hammer. The double *click* of the hammer being pulled back was ominously loud. Time seemed to stand still as awareness and fear flooded Usher's features. His eyes widened and his lower lip trembled.

Then Jamie moved, stepping quickly away from Usher.

'Don't do it,' Knight said.

Tibbs saw it in Les Usher's face, that identical anger and cruelty compounded by arrogance that had been Carleton Usher's undoing.

'You son of a bitch!'

Usher spun low, swinging his gun arm around when Knight shot him. The solitary gunshot boomed across the rocks, echoing its way to eternity. Jamie turned her head, sobbing.

Tibbs kneeled down next to Pap. The old timer had taken a terrible hit on the head, probably from Usher's gunbutt. Knight wasted no time walking out into the sage and cactus patch where he took a canteen from one of the abandoned horses. He gave Jamie the canteen and she drank greedily until Knight took the canteen away from her.

'That'll do for now. Let's get Pap fixed up.'

Tibbs and Knight cleaned the cut on Pap's head, dabbing at it with a soaked neckerchief, and then let him take a long swallow.

'Dagnabit! He pistol-whipped me!'

'You old coot, your pride's injured more than your head,' Tibbs said.

They pulled Pap to his feet.

'Let's go,' Knight said. 'There's nothing more to accomplish here.'

'What about Edgar and the other men?' Tibbs asked.

'Looks to me like the men ran off. There's no profit in being dead. And I reckon Edgar Usher will show himself soon enough. He doesn't have anywhere to go.'

In fact, Edgar Usher was waiting for them fifty yards away in the tall grass that bordered Snakebite Creek. Tibbs sensed his presence long before they saw him. They walked out of the rocks and splashed across the creek where they paused at the periphery of grass. The sandy trail that led to Raven Flats glimmered in the sun like a stark line on a map. The four of them stood appraising the trail in silence, each of them acutely aware that the final act of this tragedy was about to play out before them. Sweat trickled down their foreheads, trigger fingers itched for the pressure of metal.

Tibbs and Knight separated from the others and moved deeper into the grass. Tibbs motioned for Pap and Jamie to hold their position. The sunlight was intense, burning the desert, dismissing the warm wind. Time crawled along its molten path with a centipede's slowness.

There was movement in the brush, a whimper, and then a shout.

'Jesus! Holy mother of God!'

Then they saw a dark silhouette rise up from the grass, a rattlesnake pinned to his face, fangs imbedded in the flesh below his eye, his gun arm raised and the muzzle roaring as he fired uselessly into the sky. Edgar Usher screamed. Tearing the snake from his face he whipped it to the ground and fired four shots at the slithering diamondback before the hammer clacked hollowly on to an empty chamber.

Tibbs and Knight had their guns drawn but neither fired.

Edgar saw them, cursed, and pointed his gun at them as he fell to his knees sobbing. He pulled the hammer back and aimed at Tibbs. Again, the hammer clacked on to an empty cylinder. Pinpricks of blood had welled up on his face below his right eye. Drool flung from his lips and he raised himself up.

'Snakebite! You gotta. . . .'

He fell to his knees and began crawling. Tibbs and Knight watched in mute fascination as Edgar Usher crawled through the grass, his face already beginning to swell as the lethal venom coursed through his veins.

There was a flurry of motion as he encountered another rattlesnake. Swift as lightning the rattler struck, embedding its gleaming fangs into Edgar's thigh. He screamed again, and again. There was a frenzied burst of movement as Edgar realized that he had crawled into a nest of rattlesnakes. His screams tore at the sky and echoed across the desert.

'We'd be doing him a favor by shooting him,' Tibbs said.

'We would indeed,' Knight said.

'Except it wouldn't be legal to shoot an unarmed man.'

'No, it wouldn't be legal.'

'I figure he has about an hour,' Tibbs said.

'Maybe less.'

Then, without a backward glance, they led Pap and Jamie out of the grass and on to the trail toward town.

EPILOGUE

Feliciano and the other Mexicans pulled Carleton and Pete Usher's charred corpses from the burned remains of the mansion and then spent the afternoon collecting the bodies from town and from around Snakebite Creek. They dug the graves under the blistering noonday sun, commenting quietly to themselves on the fact that Boot Hill had doubled in size. Before a month had passed the story had gone out across the copper telegraph wires and the dime novelists began calling it, *Massacre at Snakebite Creek.* The events that had unfolded over three days that August would follow US Marshal Maxfield Knight and Deputy US Marshal Cole Tibbs for the remainder of their lives. But for Tibbs it wasn't a massacre as much as it had been a showdown, and with the reckoning done he wanted to build a new life for himself.

The following day Jamie, Pap, and Tibbs walked Knight to the train platform where the twenty ton train rested on the tracks like a metal dragon breathing steam.

'There's a group robbing trains in Kansas,' Knight said. 'When you get things settled here wire my office.'

Tibbs nodded. Knight shook Jamie's hand.

'I'm glad it's over,' she said flatly. 'There's been too much killing.'

Knight gave her an odd look, his face suddenly tense, as if he were holding something back.

'We lost thirteen thousand men at Shiloh,' Knight said. 'The Rebs lost ten thousand men. Sometimes at night I dream about Owl Creek and the water is red with blood. What happened here was a minor skirmish.'

He turned his back on them and mounted the coach stairs, brushing past the hostile conductor.

'I'm glad I'm on his side,' Pap said.

'Whatever side that is,' Tibbs said.

In moments, the train rumbled to life, steam gushing with a loud hiss and then it was on its way across the endless stretch of sand and wind and dust.

In the coming days Raven Flats became a town again. Pap Wingfoot resumed his post in his rocking chair on the boardwalk outside of his adobe cantina, smoking his pipe and watching the blackbirds in the street. Pap's yellow dog, Grant, maintained his vigil on a town that had suddenly become peaceful and didn't quite know what to do with itself. Rumors spread like wildfire that Tibbs and Jamie would marry; then rumors spread just as quickly that the engagement was cancelled as Jamie couldn't stand the violence that comes with being married to a deputy US marshal.

One afternoon Michael Keith took a break from his duties at the Fool's Gold Saloon and sat with Pap on the boardwalk.

'You think Tibbs will marry that girl?'

'Ain't got a clue.'

'It sure is quiet around here without those Usher boys

to muck things up.'

'You miss 'em?'

'Can't say that I do.'

And so it went for two weeks. Then word got around that Tibbs would ride out the next day. Early in the afternoon Pap watched Tibbs and Jamie emerge from her storefront. They walked toward him, apparently content with whatever decision they had made. They greeted Pap amiably and then Tibbs sauntered into the cantina. Pap was just as surprised as Jamie when his voice boomed out: 'Pap, get your carcass in here right now!'

Astonished, Pap and Jamie followed Tibbs into the cantina. Tibbs leaned up against the bar and slapped his palm soundly on the planks.

'Pour me a whiskey!'

Pap, with his eyes wide with surprise, said. 'I thought you only drank whiskey on Christmas or your birthday?'

'That's right,' Tibbs said with a wide grin. 'And today's my birthday!'